Dimension Surfing

Dimension Surfing

1,2,3,4, And All The Rest Of The Dimensions At Once

Bonnie Baumgartner

2007

Dimension Surfing

TABLE OF CONTENTS

Acknowledgments ix

Introduction of. xi

Glossary xv

Chapter 1 EVERYTHING is ENERGY 1
    Wellness 10
    Potentials 14
    Tug-of-war with the brain 28

Chapter 2 CHAOS THEORY 35
    History of Chaos theory 36
    What exactly is chaos 39
    Quantum physics 44
    Reality and Dimensions and Time 49

Chapter 3 *Energy EXCHANGE* and BUSINESS. 69
    SOME HISTORY FOR YOU and me. 73
    FAILURE is Part of the PROCESS 82
    BUSINESS in the New Energy 84

Chapter 4 BRAIN OVERLOAD .99
    MIND CONTROL 107
    DISSOCIATIVE Identity Disorder. 112
    AUTISM 114

A LARGE INFUSION OF SPIRITUAL
    ENERGY 120
BRAIN OVERLOAD AT DEATH 125

Chapter 5 BEING A CREATOR 133
    DENIAL 141
    VIBRATION 147
    IMAGINATION 156
    PASSION IS LOVE EXPRESSED. 159

Chapter 6 Some other ways of NEW ENERGY 167
    DEBT 175
    CHOICE 176
    Your STORY 183
    COMPROMISING 189
    The BODY we Have 194

SIGNS of starting the Ascension process. 201

OLD ENERGY ways 205

Some things we can know about NEW ENERGY. 207

my website is *www.mysticknowing.com*

ACKNOWLEDGMENTS

To the Crimson Council a celestial teaching order including:
Tobias, channeled by **Geoffrey Hoppe** *crimsoncircle.com*
Adamus Saint-Germain, channeled by **Geoffrey Hoppe** *crimsoncircle.com*
Kuthumi, channeled by **Geoffrey Hoppe** *crimsoncircle.com*

Kryon of Magnetic Service, channeled by **Lee Carroll** *kryon.com*
The Brotherhood of Light, channeled by **Edna G. Frankel** *edna@beyondreiki.com*

And all the other angels assisting us on our journey of ascension.

***

INTRODUCTION OF

DIMENSION SURFING

Your soul at play is your divine intelligence. We are souls pretending to be humans playing the game of free choice. Our circle of completion is at hand NOW. As we complete our journey of experiences ending our endless goal setting and making amends. Balancing the energy of duality that was rather lopsided is OVER. We honored the game rules **soul** had created for us.

Staying in the NOW moment we move to accepting and embracing that We Are God Also. Now we start our expansion in all directions. *We expand by creating* and living life for the sake of **pure enjoyment**. Not so easy to do. Playing and creating with all the new potentials opening up for us.

The children being born currently hold attributes humans have never held before. They are *interdimensional and capable of existing in two places at one time.* As we raise our vibrational level we are becoming interdimensional beings also, able to be in more than two places at once, surfing the dimensions.

One foot in old and the other foot in the new energy. When you change the angle you view something from you change the way it appears which changes YOUR REALITY.

The challenge is to find a way to SEE THE GIFT in **all that happens** to you and you change your reality instantly. As you become multidimensional and as the new children start coming in with these skills already embedded in them you will better understand your opportunities to move between the MANY dimensions of your experiences.

The concepts of happiness and passion, duty and service etc...Have a different definition than they did in old energy. In the new energy there is a freedom and grace that was NEVER there before. After you finish creating with the new energy you release it to grow as it wishes. That is correct creator behavior!

Energy moves in and out of the third dimension of our perceived reality in a constant state of flow that is ALWAYS available but seldom used. Energy is a *series of potentials* created in the highest realms and brought to earth as TOOLS for those who know how to bring the energy in and use it. Scientists and physicists currently on earth have a rather limited view of what energy does.

The human angels have gone through three eras on earth and are now starting their fourth. They are evolving into what they came to Earth for a *quantum leap in spiritual awareness.* The new era of Creator energy. The first group is going through now adjusting their physiology and psychology to set the template for the rest of humanity to follow when they decide to "go quantum."

There is one piece of God that you carry more of than anybody else does, a sacred contract. The collective of humanity has now reached a stage in which our sacred contract can be activated. Our sacred contracts take many forms. They may take you in a new direction for the rest of your life or they could be completed in a few minutes. Once your sacred contract is activated completed or not your soul will have satisfaction and experience a serenity and confidence while in human form.

Another rule we set up, it is not possible to identify your sacred contract until after it is done. You might never fully know what that sacred contract was. What matters is your willingness to enact the sacred contract because that is what draws it to you. You put that energy out and it finds you.

Currently we are rewiring our brain, making the two halves a whole. A heads up: When we pull aside the veil we feel a deep sadness which is disorienting because we expected joy and re-lief.

Your life DOSE have value so do not waste it any longer in the fast paced life of the third dimension of illusion.

We are **one mind** with *many thinkers*.

***

A PARTIAL GLOSSARY

The Universal Laws are all interrelated and not linear, they are in a circle. The laws can evolve and change or become obsolete because everything in the universe is energy including us.

ABUNDANCE is sustenance. Poverty and abundance are the same thing. Abundance comes when you are alone with yourself and acknowledge your divinity. When you open up and realize that everything is complete in the moment. That the moment is filled with healing, wisdom and compassion, that is abundance.

ACTION, Law of We have a choice or free will until we embrace our divinity. Where we put our attention our energy flows BUT you must ACT in order for something to start moving in that direction. Talk doesn't cut it.

ADDICTION In sacred geometry, addiction is a square of you taking in a substance or behavior, something YOU might decide is addictive. That square is sitting inside a larger square of belief. YOU *believe* you are trapped and can't get out because "it controls you." "IT" is **YOU** not taking responsibility for yourself.

During Atlantis, we built electrical grids of pleasure in the body, mind and emotions to get us to stay in our bodies. These are very much a part of us now. It is very stressful to be here and as things go faster and keep changing, we get more stressed and we seek pleasure. Addictions are in reality an extreme sensitivity to those grids of pleasure and not a sign of weakness. Addiction is a BELIEF SYSTEM many people are addicted to things like suffering or depression.

Chocolate and breathing has a soft effect on our pleasure system, sex has the most profound effect. Our pleasure centers can be shut down by not using them along with turning on our joy in life. The breath is very helpful in making the switch from pleasure to joy.

ALLOWING, law of The Universal Law of Allowing means dropping ALL judgments and ALL EMOTIONAL attachments to what others are, have or do. This is quite different from being tolerant. Tolerant is not liking what someone else is or does and you *hold negative thoughts* and let them be or do it any way. Practicing The Universal Law of Allowing requires granting to others the right to be, have and do whatever they choose.

ANGER is natural and at the deepest part of us. Anger covers hurt, frustration, and fear. Anger helps one avoid feeling pain. Anger helps to move energy and release stuck energy.

ASCENDEE Imagine all the lifetimes you have lived are in a circle around you and they have designated you in this lifetime to be the "ascendee" for all of them the "healee" for all of them. As you heal and ascend you rewrite your perception of the history of every past life you have ever had.

You are fulfilled from a soul level and you are no longer seeking to complete yourself with someone or something you and your soul ARE complete. This changes all of your interactions with other humans you no longer need them to complete you. You have gone through a period of letting go, releasing, getting sick, losing jobs and homes so you could stand firmly in the New Energy as a fulfilled BEING.

You can and might ALSO very well be the designated ascendee for all your ancestors on both sides of your family.

ASCENSION is when we keep the body we have but move to the next lifetime being fully aware of our spiritual wisdom. We are birthing our divinity within us. It represents a divine energy by the human who takes the hand of soul and never lets go. We become an observer OUTSIDE of duality. Our Free Will is now embraced by Divine Will and we become a divine human.

You do not give your energy (power) away to anyone else, you are sovereign. For each ascension level we release our agendas and judgments or set them aside. We move from who we thought we were to NO identity. From going through "spiritual depression" and voids now and again to embrace an ever expanding identity, we increase what we remember. This process causes sadness and doubt in us because it is new and different and we grieve for who we were.

Ascension is a state of grace reached through clearing and balancing all of our layers; physical, emotional, mental and spiritual. A shift in consciousness from duality to oneness. Along the way we learn to work and play with childlike enthusiasm in the now moment.

We take control of our biology and chronological age. We rewrite our contract, vibrating higher and living a longer life. Some of us will even change names and actually become a different person.

Ascension is the energy of the masters who walked the earth and told you that you could be just like them.

ATLANTIS *or* ALT existed for thousands of years. Shaumbra worked in the temples of Tien (present day Cuba). They were scientists doing energy and healing work. They lived in two dimensions one of which was invisible.

Towards the end of the time of Atlantis a rather mean spirited ruler took over. His name was Azure Tamu, (blue hues to his skin) "all mighty" (many times worse than Hitler) took over and tortured people physically. Tamu also used mental abuse and implants as a form of government programming. He tore apart families and eventually unbalanced the planet and destroyed Atlantis.

ATTRACTION, Law of The Universal Law of attraction says our feelings, words, thoughts and actions produce energies which in turn attract THE SAME energies on the same frequencies to us. We get back more of what we put out.

BLESSINGS are energies in a potential state waiting to be activated. Awareness opportunities or synchronicities that your soul orchestrates for you to increase your consciousness.

COMPASSION is feeling whole and complete honoring and accepting without condition. Compassion is strong and thick for any experience we are having.
Respect is incomplete compassion.
Compassion creates an INTERDIMENSIONAL ACTION and increases your light. Compassion is the catalyst for change. It is the one connection that each one of you has.

COMPROMISE In duality we often compromise our energy and mind so much that the person appears stubborn because they do not know which direction to go. We fragment and split ourselves when we are not true to ourselves. The time for compromise IS OVER. Searching outside ourselves for answers is compromise. We need to be true to ourselves. In the new energy when you hold back because you are compromising, it will be exposed anyway. Looking outside yourself for answers makes your energy drop which puts you back into old energy, duality.

CONSPIRACY is a joining together of ideals, goals and thoughts.

CRIMSON CIRCLE The group of humans involved in this spiritual journey in the New Energy preparing to become teachers to others on their journey.

CRIMSON COUNCIL Educators giving themselves in service. They have studied the SPIRITUAL aspects of entities on both sides of the veil. They go to unexplored physical and none physical dimensions or places of consciousness and asses them and how they operate. Then they report back to the Angels to teach that information to others and how to deal with the new energies.

DEATH leaving your physical body behind and transitioning to a different level of consciousness. 80% of those that die get lost in the forth dimension frequently and start the cycle of taking a body and going back to the forth dimension and ultimately staying earth bound. Of those that keep cycling from a body to forth dimension only ten percent are able to evolve out of that and get to the bridge of flowers on there own without help.

DEPRESSION CAN BE used as a fuel to ascension.

Human depression that is not related to the ascension process is about this lifetime. It is getting into a very low energy wave a slow vibration. Usually the person is absorbed in HATING of themselves. Depression is an addiction to hanging onto and wallowing in the pain of their old story.

The depressed person will get energized by talking about themselves and their suffering in THEIR STORY. A story about what they should be...What they ought to accomplish... and their SUPPRESSED anger at the self creates the depression. One of the reasons not to judge yourself where is the benefit?

Releasing your *expectations* can release the depression. A sadness about something in your life can move into a depression. Depression can last three months to all lifetime or something in between.

DIVINE INTUITION Is a guidance system that helps you to know how fast to go and which way to turn. You will not get this information in advance you get it in the now moment when you need it.

DIVINE WILL Loving acceptance of all things.

DIVINITY is the most pure essence and innocent energy. Fruit of the Rose is our divinity the part of God we brought with us. The energy of the solution is always present in our divinity.

DUALITY Everything we have experienced on Earth until now has been seen through the illusion of duality. All our perceptions have been clouded by the veil of forgetfulness. This includes what we see with our physical eyes to our highest spiritual truths. We have been living our lives and making our decisions or creating our relationships and following our goals under a very diminished reality system and using far lesser truths. Duality gains its energy from separation and opposing poles like male or female, good or bad, dark or light.

EMBRACE is to hold tenderly. When you choose opposition your divinity will wait for your embrace. The embrace is the way your divinity will join you. If you do not embrace life you will not have potentials. Embrace but do not strangle your experience or get bogged down with the details.

EMBODYING is coming to terms with and a fearless acceptance of **All That Is** without walls, barriers or judgment. Being brave enough to feel all the different energies while understanding that you will NEVER lose your identity or integrity while feeling other energies. The Kingdom of God literally lies within your torso and heart. It is your divine spark and connection to your soul.

ENERGY essentially is in a neutral state of being and is a potential waiting to be expressed through our imagination. It has many layers.

EXPANDED MOMENT allows you to be fully present right now AND allows you to expand into other realms and dimensions to feel and be aware of many other things around you all in the same moment. The expanded moment is NOW time and not linear.

FEARS as we walk through our personal fears we transmute them to LOVE energy. When we say we are ready for a change, any change FEAR comes in to challenge our change. All things have an energy consciousness. When questioning the unseen world demand the answer come from truth and love. When you talk to it you are owning and embracing it because you let it express itself. You listened to your fear and converted the energy to something useful for you.

FIRST CIRCLE is Home the original creation of God or is referred to as the First Creation. This is where we came from before embarking on this journey for Spirit. When we went through the wall of fire and into the void and started the illusion of duality the first split of our oneness was into male and female.

FREE WILL the ability to make your own personal choices. As we embrace our divinity we surrender to our divine will.

GOD is a reflection of the human consciousness. As a leader is a reflection of its followers. God is unconditional love, compassion the "is-ness." God has a presence within you and all around you. **You are God also** in a different way than the God of Home. God is ALWAYS creating as an expression of love.

HEALING is only *wisdom.* The future is the past healed. Healing is the balancing of your energy.

HOLOGRAM Imagine that there is another earth out there floating around. It is nothing more than a hologram where two or more sources of light cross each other and create a three dimensional image in space. That is what a hologram is, intersecting points of light. The Earth and ALL we see as physical began as a hologram of light. The light source is your own thoughts, passion, ideas and concepts and when a whole bunch of people focus their concepts a new hologram of light is created. It becomes a thought of god, a manifestation that you, yourselves have created. What eventually happens is the hologram gets so strong it will overlay the original hologram.

HUMAN the 10% of us which is temporarily wired into a carbon-based physical life form. Humans are here to transmute matter from a lower vibratory level to a higher vibration of existence. This necessitates a physical body from the third dimension to pass as a gateway through which only the higher energy can rise. In order for this transmutation of matter to be accomplished it needed to be done by a consciousness that had forgotten who it was, that would be the human. We had forgotten our eternal Beingness and our vast presence as angels within the body of God.

INFORMATION is building and being downloaded into us. Then being stored in us until we can understand it or want to access it.

IMAGINATION is the intelligence of the new energy and is used by the creator to create with. There is no right or wrong. Your imagination can MOVE into and *through* all the DIMENSIONS and can solve challenges. Imagination is in your tool kit and the use of the imagination is how we explore all our available probabilities so we can pick which ones we want to expand and develop. Integrate compassion into your being and your imagination goes off to see what is going on everywhere, it senses the many layers that surround you. Imagination is in a NEW TYPE of FLOW and when you send out for people or supplies they come to you.

KARMA simply means an energetic type of influence or balance.

KNOWINGNESS or gnost is NOT known to the brain. Knowingness comes from other dimensions or realms as your essence does, it is a type of dream or imagination state. Going to that state will allow you to bring that information or essence into the third dimension and after grounding it here it starts transforming itself into an energy that eventually will be understood by the mind. That is where breakthroughs and "ahas" come from.

LOVE total compassion, strong and thick for any experience we had and are having.

MASTERY is taking something that has become negative in your life and finding a positive uses for it. That is the process called mastery. Mastery is when you are not fearful and you are peaceful when others are not, you do not do drama. A human's first reaction is to fight when provoked. A master's first reaction is to check herself to see if her integrity is in place.

METATRON our collective voice in Spirit. In the new energy there is a new consciousness and vibration on Earth that allows the integration of our divine nature into our human nature.

NEW ENERGY is expansional and moves in and out of dimensions. There is an infinite supply of energy available. In oneness there are no opposing forces. Imagination is used to create with. We have seen such a small bit of what is true, now we will see a vastly larger picture. Our DNA loops will begin working together again. As they do that, it will help to heal all of our past wounds and scars within our body, emotions and mind, along with reversing the aging process. There is only NOW interdimensional time. In the new energy there will be a compassion and the giving and receiving of unconditional love as a state of timeless serenity.

A higher vibration will eliminate the pain and suffering. There is enough abundance and compassion available for everyone. Though as creators we will feel FEAR and *self doubt* we will understand those emotions are real and present and the energies do not need to be considered **negative** they can work with YOU and for your creations.

New Energy is a potential. It is very present in your life right now. It's as much in the Now as your perception of yourself is. It's here with you. You haven't necessarily seen it or felt it, because it cannot be defined. It's undefinable with the current tools and resources we have for defining things.

<u>90%ER</u> refers to the invisible parts of the human which is only 10% of the conglomerate we are

<u>OMNI- PHYSICS</u> all the potentials and their behaviors. Envision the potentials as bubbles that exist outside of physical reality waiting to be brought into physical reality. Each bubble on its own, representing a different potential. As the human brings things into reality the literal bubbles of potential gather together, as atoms do in all the molecules of our scientific structures. They are attracted to what you are choosing in your life and begin to come in. Sometimes they cluster all around you in a state of potential waiting for expression, reality turning into matter, opportunity or concept finding their way to you.

OVERSOUL is a collective of all of the energies of everything you have been.

The higher self functions as a big river with little streams. Each higher self manages around twelve life threads at a time. Each oversoul manages a dozen higher selves at a time. The sacred mathematics of 12 x 12 = 144. A soul family is about a "gross" of souls, just like a gross of beads. When one life ends it is feed to another life energy, one of the threads. No energy is ever lost or wasted!

PASSION is love expressed, expansive and open to all the many new realms. Passion is fuel. If you are not so sure what to do sit in a quiet moment and feel what passion has to say. The answer of knowingness will come to you. When we attempt to control new energy passion with old human ways it will hurt us.

SACRED GEOMETRY is sacred to the observer or discoverer of the geometric shapes. The term has been used to encompass the religious, philosophical and spiritual beliefs that have sprung up around geometry in various cultures during the course of human history. The ancients believed that the experience of sacred geometry was essential to the education of the SOUL. Math follows the consciousness of humans.

SECOND CIRCLE Everything outside of the First Circle. The realm in which we as humans live. The consciousness we are responsible for creating and shaping. Also referred to as the Second Creation.

SHOUD the collective energy and voice of each and everyone speaking as one.

SHAUMBRA There are many layers of this. At its simplest level shaumbra means family. We are back with our extended family across this Earth. The second portion of this "ba-rah" has to do with experience, journey and mission. So when this energy is put together, it is "shau-home-ba-rah" which means family that is on a journey and experiencing it together.

The code that was used at the time of Yeshua ben Joseph (Jesus) was a type of garment, a scarf or shawl that was worn by either male or female. It was the distinctive color of crimson that let the others of family know it was time to meet. Many of them Essences would gather for secret spiritual meetings.

The group of humans going through the awakening process.

SILICON Many forms of life contain silicon structures (biogenic silica), including microorganisms such as diatoms, plants such as horsetail, and animals such as hexactinellid sponges. It is present in the cell walls of various plants (including edible ones) to strengthen their structural integrity.

Our carbon based bodies get threaded with silicon when we are in the void and as our awareness increases, your silicon increases.

SOUL Is our unique individual unified identity of the self. Soul understands every probability and potential and the shadow potentials. Soul is everything we have done or been and thought the rest is discovery.

In my books I use the term soul to include what we call spirit, holy ghost, higher self, etc.... and all the other invisible aspects of ourselves.

The soul is an identity, a very unique identity. Soul is the expression of what you would call God or Spirit. The soul is your I AM, the overview of all that is visible and invisible, a divine wholeness. Your soul cannot be defined or structured or controlled. Soul has not been able to, or wanted to come into a limited, overly structured and suppressive environment where the mind rules and reality is inflexible.

SPIRIT is the same as the higher self, awareness, life force, I am, expression of God. Spirit goes to earth THROUGH the Human to manifest "spirits" beliefs, to see how they play out. Our energy as humans is always broadcasting our life in real time to all entities in the universe.

SPIRITUAL DEPRESSION is not caused by the MIND and the mind is NOT involved. When we grab the hand of soul and take THE LEAP OF FAITH, or the dark night of the soul, a spiritual metamorphosis or transmutation is taking place. The transitional state between going from human to becoming a **divine human angel**. You will experience spiritual NUMBNESS and feel abandoned by God at this time. The irony is your soul is as close to you as it is possible to be. You are in between, in a dark hole moving from the caterpillar state to becoming a butterfly, the chrysalis stage. This is the final release or surrender of your human beliefs and ways.

BREATHE it in and bring in the compassion for yourself. This depression has been building up for many lifetimes and is part of the ascension process. The first time ever that we have done this while having a body.

The tears and stories come tumbling out.

Depression and ascension are an interrelated process. You are dying, letting go of the old limiting story you created and have built for many many lifetimes. Now is the time to release the story so the energy can be transmute and made available to you in a new way.

When you breathe you start feeling, LIVING and waking UP. Spiritual depression generally lasts a year. During that time you will slip in and out of the void. It is the time things and people start to go away.

When the human REJECTS the spiritual depression (SOUL) the human slips into a third dimensional depression.

Depression is used as a fuel to ascension.

10%er or the human which is only ten percent of the whole.

TIME is roundish and not linear like the illusion on earth. Time can be expanded or compressed to suit our need. Time speeds up as our consciousness increases and slows down when our awareness slows down. Basically there is no time. Time is an artificial creation by humans to help understand how to get from one moment to the next in their daily journey. Time is just a belief system that you have divided energy into. In reality, and definitely in the other realms what we call time is a sequence of events that takes place. A sequence of what unseen world calls points of separation that take place. A series of choices or sequences that build one upon the other. But because the final choice has already been made, the sequence of events is just walking backwards through time.

THIRD LANGUAGE is a metaphor for our communication with spirit or soul. It happens naturally and slowly inside us. It can be the feedback feeling that may wash over us like a tingle or a touch on the head. It feels like shiveries to me. That feeling means that we have reached a place where we can feel and experience the energy of compassion which activates communication and we feel the feedback of the soul energy or any of our other invisible parts wash over us.

TRUTH is always evolving you never find it except on some of the higher angelic realms. When you try to change the world with YOUR truth it try's to change you.

WALL OF FIRE A metaphor for "doorway" leading from Home into the Void which is now our universe. The zone we crossed through going from the First Circle to the Second Circle.

VOID or a Null Zone is established after there has been an expansion outwards of energy which receives a blow or shock causing it to collapse inwards upon itself. The old established **energy patterns have now been broken.** There is no way that they will ever return to their previous patterning. They have been irrevocably changed. The energy of a Null Zone feels jagged and raw. There is much hurt and pain. You find most EVERYTHING irritates you even other people breathing is irritating. It's the shattering of a world or a belief system, a long-held desire, or sometimes an important relationship with yourself or another.

You experience the feeling with your heart first. Then the brain processes the experience. The old belief cast in stone gets shattered.

This would be similar to the feeling you would have after being in a hurricane or any natural disaster. This shattering creates the perfect foundation for the introduction of something ENTIRELY new to come in. The potential is enormous. Null Zones or voids **AMPLIFY** and *destabilize* whatever inherent discord is present in the surrounding areas. They actually occur to help us break free from old stagnant patterns and belief systems giving us a unique opportunity for a quantum leap into a deeper sector of the unknown.

While in the void a lot of MENTAL and EMOTIONAL processing is done. Processing and new perspectives on past and present life belief systems happen in the void. The void is a womb to birth the new in.

Generally voids last a few months or can be a few weeks.

The Void is also the nothingness outside of the Kingdom, or First Creation. The consciousness we ventured into to discover something new for Spirit that could not be known within the First Creation.

***

CHAPTER I

EVERYTHING is ENERGY

The "age of new energy" is here right now!

The energy has been arriving for the past twenty years and has a few years left to complete delivery. Energy moves in and out of the third dimension of our perceived reality in a constant state of flow that is ALWAYS available but seldom used. Energy is a series of potentials created in the highest realms and brought to earth as tools for those who know how to bring the energy in and use it. Scientists and physicists currently on earth have a rather limited view of what energy does.

The **first place** we feel the new energy is in our mind and body. This energy has been ALLOWED in easily and simply. We no longer need two opposing forces to create new energy. For a while, possibly several generations, old and new energy will be present on earth together. Old energy resides pretty heavily in some people and places.

<u>NEW ENERGY</u> is expansional and moves in and out of dimensions. There is an infinite supply of energy available. In oneness there are no opposing forces. Imagination is used to create with. We have seen such a small bit of what is true, now we will see a vastly larger picture. Our DNA loops will begin working together again. As they do that, it will help to heal all of our past wounds and scars within our body, emotions and mind, along with reversing the aging process. There is only

NOW interdimensional time. In the new energy there will be a compassion and the giving and receiving of unconditional love as a state of timeless serenity.

A higher vibration will eliminate the pain and suffering. There is enough abundance and compassion available for everyone. Though as creators we will feel FEAR and *self doubt* we will understand those emotions are real and present and the energies do not need to be considered **negative** they can work with YOU and for your creations.

New Energy is a potential. It is very present in your life right now. It's as much in the Now as your perception of yourself is. It's here with you. You haven't necessarily seen it or felt it, because it cannot be defined. It's undefinable with the current tools and resources we have for defining things.

***

The humans have gone through three eras on earth and the fourth era starts now. We are in completion of what we came to Earth to do. We gave Earth life and we are known as the Family of the Rock.

First was the age of **LEMURIA.**

Second was *ATLANTIS*, lasting thousands of years.

Third is the **CHRISTOS** era which is ending as we leave duality with our spiritual awareness greatly increased.

Fourth is the age of our DIVINITY and Creator energy with a new and expanded consciousness moving into *oneness or unity*. Our entire solar system is going into the new energy. The template has been set for the entire world and the rest of humanity to follow when they decide to "go quantum." The first group that has gone through ascension has a wealth of experience to offer the next group and they are still learning more than they thought it was possible to learn.

Humans will continue to go through many, many challenges on their way to the new energy and through this metamorphosis. The whole transformation period from 1987 to September 2007 or 2012 has grounded the potential for EVERYTHING to change. We will have the ability to make easier, faster changes in every aspect of OUR lives.

You can choose to embrace this energy now, there is not reason to wait. Then expect the POTENTIAL of change for everything. Peace on Earth could even breakout. Our awareness is speeding up and evolving so quickly we will literally leave our old systems and cycles while we move into whole new systems.

The first place you will notice changes will be in your consciousness. The changes happen as the seen and unseen parts of you start working together. No longer will the human feel isolation they are getting to know there unseen aspects. There is a different you evolving, the human 10%er, working with its invisible 90%er in collaboration.

As the collaboration starts functioning as a unit and unfolding in your life, it might be a bit clumsy and jarring. The changes come so fast your biology could struggle trying to keep up. Your body and mind do not work like they used to work because a lot of retraining is going on and will become permanent. Learning new ways and concepts in all aspects of your life can be rather disconcerting until you adjust to the changes that beget more change and even greater changes than EVER before. Know that none of the new change has been generated by the human self.

OLD ENERGY: new awareness happens VERY slowly. The same amount of energy keeps being recycled. The biblical times are ending. A large number of birds and some animals will be leaving, as their time of service to us is over, they want to go home. Duality is a template of consciousness requiring separation. The separation is between awareness of the physical body and the etheric body. Your etheric body is your link to "All That Is" and you are (have been) consciously disconnected from it.

NEW ENERGY comes into the individual, altering the body and mind to a higher spiritual level. Change is rapid and awareness is increasing and evolving. Instead of turning to the Bible or other religious text, people will go inside themselves for answers. We are INSIDE and OF God, a oneness. The new energy is incorruptible. There are many more potentials and larger amounts of energy available than there ever has been before.

Once you ALLOW the new energy to enter, change is rapid.

You notice that you loose track of time and your spacial orientation gets fluid.

There *will be spiritual house cleaning* and during that time you will want to have more **"alone time"** to get to know your NEW combined self better.

There is nothing to be fearful about and if you get fearful it will slow or stop your expansion. The new energy is safe, remind yourself over and over again THE NEW ENERGY IS SAFE, go with the flow. The new expanded energy CANNOT be misused. Greedy and corrupt people cannot unbalance the new energy. No human can use their light or energy to steam roll another human. The new energy CANNOT be **owned**, HOARDED or *manipulated*.

Have you noticed more depression or strange behavior going on around you?

Much of it is the result of having our brains rewired. The rewiring starts now for all humans. Many "light workers" have been going through the rewiring for the past five years. Compassion will be needed more than ever before. There is always chaos when humans are confronted with change.

Everything is the journey **there IS NO DESTINATION.**

Our 90%er is rewiring and reworking the human brain and DNA , reconnecting all twelve loops. This is an evolutionary cycle, nothing awful is happening. The brain needed to be separated to give humans the illusion of aloneness in duality. The veil exists between the two halves of the brain. We have made the veil so thick we have forgotten we are spirits or souls.

The *left side* of the brain marks linear time and gives us the game we are playing. The left side pretends to be human and quantifies everything and puts it in boxes. Human thinks it is "human" when it is only soul playing a game. See how creative soul has been with us.

Right side is the creative brain with the concept of NOW time. The right side of the brain is infinite because it is God, You Are God Also. It is our soul moving into the human that is causing our biology to change in order to accommodate it.

We are playing this game to define or see God because in an infinite state God cannot study itself. By wearing a body we are the definition of God. We are not the only God there are many on the planet. As you vibrate higher everyone around you matches your vibration. This is a good thing, fear not as fear is only the energy of the unknown once "you know" fear leaves. Only the highest vibrating angels came to earth at this time.

We exist in twelve different dimensions at the same time and are having twelve slightly different experiences as one soul. Twelve different expressions of one soul on this planet simultaneously. What if you left one life in one dimension and went to another dimension to consult with another part of your soul for answers or awareness to an issue you had. Your path was laid out for you by you. We need to adjust our rather limited thoughts.

Your first experience with multidimensionality can cause you to lose your grounding and possibly get you stuck between energetic dimensions. There are times the physical body needs grounding to keep you here on earth. When the body is not grounded enough for the rewiring process it will overload the body. Then the hypothalamus gland overproduces and the ungrounded physical body produces illnesses like Chronic Fatigue Syndrome and Fibromyalgia. These energy disorders and are likely to increase in the general population in the next few years. Your 90%er might create one of theses energetic illnesses because you cannot move forward until you have fully received the gift of your illness.

As the rewiring in the brain takes place many people will experience unexplained headaches or dizziness that they never had before. This is a normal process and there is nothing to fear. Know that fear makes your symptoms get more pronounced. The law of like attracting like, attracts similar energy. See a doctor if you are worried in any way. Use and honor all the flavors of truth and choose those best for you.

Many people will have uncommon or unexplained respiratory system changes and challenges over the next five years. As these changes happen many of you will see them as allergies or colds. Allergies and colds that do not follow a normal path and will calm down as your new wiring is adapted into your physical form. As the rewiring progresses your patterns will change. All of these changes will NOT produce negative results. As you set these things into motion you start expecting new things from yourself.

We are here to work with each other on this planet. To teach and learn from each other, to heal and be healed, to love each other unconditionally. We are all looking for the same answers to the same questions. Now is the time to step into your power and destiny.

Seek balance in all areas of your life; that means plenty of hugs, touching other humans, feeding and resting your body and soul. This means paying attention to the beauty surrounding us. There are times the physical body needs grounding to keep your body on earth. When the body is not grounded enough for re-wiring the process will overload the body.

*Do not forget to laugh it is all **just a game**.*

As we pull aside the veil we might feel a deep sadness which is disorienting because we expected joy and relief.

As we become increasingly in tune with the invisible movements around us, feeling them flow, they will slowly start to come into focus and physical matter will start to fade, becoming increasingly unreal and transparent. In the subtle realms more can be achieved with less effort. Space flows and is as alive as water is.

We even have an invisible layer of DNA that helps us to remember all of our conglomerate parts. If you desire to activate that layer, ask your 90%er to please "make it so" because you are ready to remember. If you remember now or later, it does not matter because sooner or later your human self will become aware of all its other invisible aspects, including our divine aspect.

DNA is not in strand form. All twelve loops, two visible and ten invisible, are in LOOP form, like time is. DNA transmits electricity with the same attributes of a highly cooled wire. Our DNA is loops of code with a consistent but often unique current flowing through them setting up a small magnetic field which allows for the transfer of information through magnetism.

As the veil between the seen and unseen gets thinner and thinner in us, we will become increasingly aware of all our invisible parts and how they work together in concert with each other and the human. Humans each have their own individual veil as part and parcel of their body and the 90%er controls the veil's density.

Trying to make our bodies less dense to accommodate the new energy requires rewiring of our bodies down to our invisible DNA. Our bodies direct themselves and don't need our participation in order to function. The biology DOES like to be honored for its hard work.

Sleeping in a twenty-four hour period will change into a triad of sleep, three spots of sleep interrupted twice, all part of the new vibration or energy . This will eventually become our new normal sleep pattern.

The clearer the body is of stuck spots and trauma to its aura and physical parts, the easier it is for the body to vibrate higher. When we vibrate higher we have the ability to blend with higher faster energy waves.

Our spiritual awakening is a large amount of rapid change, creating a sadness and grief as we leave behind all we are familiar with. Another reason why we feel emotional and sorrowful is because we are also saying goodbye to the large group of souls we have traveled with in an astral way for eons of time. Our karmic groups or families have traveled with us through our many incarnations with our many overlapping ages, deaths and births.

FOR THE FIRST time in human existence we are allowed to step out of these groups on our own, while we are still in bodies.

We came into this lifetime with multiple contracts and many were carried over from our past lives. We do not have conscious awareness of what the contracts are any longer. If you want to know about your contracts and are in communication with your 90%er, just ask. They will be happy to tell you.

On the other side of the veil there are always new planning sessions for our contracts or agreements. We are interdimensional and attend the meetings, but it is questionable how much we remember. It would be good if they E-mailed the human the minutes from those meetings!

Some people are locked into compulsive busyness or dissociation to avoid how they feel. They avoid ALL feelings, good and bad. They might not realize they are also shutting down their VERY OWN life force and eventually will shut down their life. By embracing numbness, a depressive sadness takes over. The universe, trying to please them, gives them more of what they APPEAR to be enjoying. Numbness embraces them with or without any addiction or drug use.

Humans that decide in advance how things *SHOULD* be and when they should happen will be very frustrated because things will go down a different way or not at all the way they decided "it should be." Work on relinquishing the control you have always needed to "make things happen." Let go of what you expect things to look like. Allow expansion in ways that far exceed your vision.

We were to learn about and USE **compassion**, *acceptance* and NONJUDGMENT with each other. A feeling or a glance can convey volumes of knowledge. In the new energy, we can move slower but achieve a great deal more without the struggles of duality. There is a new sense of serenity when you are aligned with the new energy or your soul. A great sense of detachment takes over. You also gain a generalized feeling of love.

You feel different. Your focus changes from the material world to the invisible worlds or dimensions. When your soul and you work together you are in the flow, things start to clean up in your life. You will experience going into a void periodically as your body moves to a new internal grid pattern. The silicon threads are implanted and grow within you, making your body lighter and not in need of as much maintenance as it needed before. Eventually you will require less sleep and food. Synchronicities occur with increasing frequency as you work with your 90%er. Things get easier. Old issues and upsets dissolve away faster without the deep wounding you might have taken on in the past.

As we move from brain control to universal intelligence, your 90%er will give you a poke before your intellect can analyze your intuition away or negate it. The unseen world uses human emotion as a conduit for those that let themselves feel. When you get poked, ask questions out loud to minimize confusion. When you are grateful, they like you to share that, out loud is best.

It is the human way to think you need to work hard for what you have. Your 90%er says you have deserved gifts waiting for you. Just being here as a human is the hard work. The details of what you get and when are not controlled by the human it is controlled by soul.

When we walk into our fears and transmute them, we are bringing a love and light balance to a great portion of the entire universe. The vibration of this planet is driven by many things we cannot fathom. The vibration has been **neutral** and NOT LIGHT or DARK for eons and eons.

✵✵✵

Wellness

Most of you are healers. "Healer, heal thyself." means "practice what you preach." If you are going to facilitate others to grow and heal then seek growth and healing yourself. True healers are usually in the process of healing themselves at the same time as those they facilitate. In the past, we let "others" heal us or be in charge of our healing. At times, we even tried to force healing. In the new energy, we need to TAKE ON the responsibility for **healing ourselves**. We can only balance each other. Certainly others can assist but canNOT do it for you. In the new energy a healer does not have the "job to heal" only a job to create space for others to feel comfortable enough to heal themselves.

At some level you might fear healing because in a past life you may have burned at the stake when other humans feared your knowledge. Humans only fear things that they do not understand. Fear is a lack of light and knowledge. Fill in the knowledge and fear releases.

It's time to incorporate our biology in our enlightenment. When speaking of a body part, use "we" because all of our parts are one unit. Greet your food BEFORE you put it in your mouth. That way the body is ready and you give your body permission for all your parts to work together for their highest good.

Is it appropriate to turn a light on in a dark room? Do you force the occupant to see? No, you enable them to choose. Is it appropriate to balance without permission from the biology and having its cooperation?

Our cell structure SINGS a *certain tune* to keep the body alive and well. It vibrates at well above 100,000 vibrations per second. The cell structure sings in **harmony** to get healing and create miracles.

Talk to your cells because your enlightenment is not in your head. Every single cell knows everything. The more we talk to our cellular structure about who we are and our divinity, the more communication we'll have with our soul and the higher dimensions.

The new energy speeds up the process of releasing things that want to be released and rebalanced so healing is faster and simpler. NO force at all need be used. The new energy seeks balance, so to heal people there is no need for potions or drama. Every human that is imbalanced or unconscious has a piece of pure balance in EVERY CELL. When the brain is in dysfunction, quite often the other cells are fine and yelling for balance. Our cells do NOT NEED the brain to become balanced.

ARE YOU READY TO HEAL?

Do you need help healing?

Ask a compassionate friend willing to help you. Your friend will help you see the potentials available to you. Your healer friend creates a mood that will relax the mind and body so you feel safe. Your healer is holding a space for you to see the potentials that will allow your body to rebalance. Any DOUBTS the healer has WILL stand in the way of rebalancing.

Our bodies were designed to live over 900 years.

The invisible realm is reawakening our thymus which in turn changes our DNA so we can live longer and decide WHEN we want to die. Spontaneous healing is the consciousness of love over physics.

We are shifting from our immune system to the thymus for protection. Our immune system FIGHTS an enemy in our body. Our thymus **EMBRACES** an enemy in our body and *transmutes THE ENEMY into harmony.* In the new energy, our thymus will use its energy and wisdom to bring an invader to a place of harmony and common purpose.

A poison becomes a healing substance when love is added. The new energy we created is the power of love. There is no negative entity or thing we cannot change with love. Now we are completely in control of events and the direction BUT not the details. Our cosmic intelligence knows best.

Death from disease will happen less and less.

Your body is a product of your THOUGHTS.

Disease is held in the body by your *thoughts and feelings* of **rejection** and CONTROL which in turn is forced on the body. Your thoughts will create the imbalance in your body and your body will then manifest the imbalance. Do you want to alter the body's balance? Redirect your awareness to figure out what thoughts created the imbalance.

Certain diseases are connected with certain thought patterns. Heart problems are from rejection of your divine self. Diabetes is the inability to get the sweetness from life. You need to give yourself the sweetness. Calcium deposits are from withholding your love. Are you waiting to be sure you get your love first before you part with your love?

What might be a problem with that reasoning, besides calcium deposits and expecting others to read your mind?

When the masters walked the earth and healed people, they must have been masters of compassion first and healers second. Compassion starts with you having compassion for yourself. Before you can embody love, you need to master giving and RECEIVING love, most humans weak area. Mastery demands a scenario of purity that is very attainable because it is built into our DNA and is very ready to be activated at this time.

OLD ENERGY: Law of Conservation of Energy—energy can neither be created nor destroyed. Energy can be converted from one form into another. Third dimensional time and space are linear. We offered our body up for others to heal on our behalf.

NEW ENERGY: Is the new quantum interdimensional physics. New energy is expansional, and there is an infinite supply available. The speed of light is VARIABLE from time frame to time frame. Any rules are unique to each reality or dimension. There is only "NOW" interdimensional time. We are now in charge of healing ourselves.

Speaking with your cells is an *ENERGETIC* process, your cells do not understand ANY language. Energy is what is needed. Visualize, do not verbalize to your cells. Spend time addressing your cells with the visualization of what you want. Imagine yourself with young DNA. The body went through that and has a cellular memory of your young DNA. Communicate daily for just a few minutes, creating a strong visions of what the goal is for your body process. See young skin, young health, and a young attitude. Your body will get the idea and begin to conform what you showed it.

❈❈❈

Potentials

All the many, many potentials and probabilities CHANGE their *vibration and energy* constantly. Different parts separate and reunite with other bits just like a grand square dance on steroids. The partners have no idea who they will be dancing with next. FREQUENTLY it is the human that precipitates the change and not the unseen world. When you notice changes and shifts, DO take credit for them. They are coming from the expanded human and not from someone or something else. The human is reaching into their pastlives to get all their skill sets hooked up together. Humans are integrating their old and new knowledge of things. They are coming up with awareness' they never had in the past.

TAKE credit for all you have put together to create the expanded now.

In quantum physics, you the creator can't have a universe without your FEELINGS and THOUGHTS affecting the outcomes. Our feelings and passion shape our thoughts about what is being perceived and created. The heart and then the mind shapes our world. Nothing can be viewed in linear time and space any longer.

NO LONGER **can things be added up in a** LINEAR WAY.

When you have a feeling, your mind tries to decipher a meaning and definition of your feeling. Then your mind wants to TAKE an action for you. Yes, the mind is a control freak and sometimes sees danger when there isn't any. The mind is rather limited in its awareness. Is that what you want running your life?

Your current behaviors and thoughts **do** create your future.

Your current behaviors and thoughts have a *vibration* that RESONATES out from you. Take a look at what you are resonating out and tell me what you see, my dear? Is it pretty, bright and sparkly? Long and skinny, or round and tight? Do people get a headache from what you resonate and have they run away and hidden or do they smile back at you or maybe you have become invisible?

If you have round, skinny, tight things in your life, that is because your frequency magnetically attracts other things and people that also resonate at the round, skinny, tight thing frequency. You get more and more of what you put out. Just like a boomerang.

Crabby begets crabby and criticism begets more criticism. To change what shows up in your life you will need a frequency change. I trust you would want to move to a higher vibration level. Sadly you cannot order a higher vibration on line, it needs to be created by your OWN self. Shocking as it sounds, one of the best ways to do that is have compassion for YOURSELF. I know, for some that seems an impossible challenge. You do realize that is because you are judging yourself.

When you say "I AM NOT" or "I CANNOT" you create what you aren't and can't do. No outside force is taking that from you. YES, you took it from yourself. What you lack or can't do you took away from you. Is that the limitation you want to hold close and tight?

When you say, "I hate and will NOT accept what was done to me," you are bringing down your vibration.

I will grow and nurture this hate until it is 80% of who I am, a walking angry wound. Along with that, I get the bonus prize of a greatly lowered vibration.

Or was the hateful thing done to me as a "test" I created for myself to see if I could rise above it and have compassion for myself?

Manifesting is manifesting!

There is no judgment put on it by the universe. It is only a bit of physics. Like attracting like energy. Manifesting is *one tool* in our tool kit to explore and play with. If we want to manifest hate and draw more hate to us, "you go girl."

The Law of Attraction: Our feelings, words, thoughts, and actions produce energies which in turn attract THE SAME energies on the same frequencies. Consider becoming what you want more of. Release what you do not want in order to gain something new that you do want.

A word of caution: you cannot put new on top of the old because the old will still come through. Create an action plan for yourself to release what you have experienced enough of, like poverty, drama or criticism.

If you feel so inclined, ask the invisible realm to show you an incident that demonstrates to you what you are doing that you want to release so it is very clear in your mind and heart. Ask for any tips or help they can give to get you separated from what you want to release. Ask if there is a block you are not aware of that needs to be addressed first. Frequently your awareness and honesty with yourself will release whatever game you played with yourself to increase your wisdom.

Integrate each new bit of awareness with what you already know.

Open up to your soul for inspiration and guidance. I use the word "soul" to represent all of your aspects in the invisible realm like spirit, higher self, awareness, life force, I AM, expression of God.

Soul comes to earth **THROUGH** the human to manifest the beliefs of our invisible parts and see how they play out in our denseness. Yes, it is all a learning experience, so lighten up and have fun with it. Like you did with your "legos" or your crayons, fire up your imagination and have fun.

Can you see the GIFT in the experiences you have created for yourself to learn from? Focus on WHAT IS present in your life and be grateful for that. Appreciation pulls in more of the same. Have gratitude for being healthy and whole. Energy flows where your attention goes.

Your actions and feelings and thoughts need to be consistent and back each other up. If you are *acting* out an addiction and *feeling* disjointed and *thinking* about financial wealth, there is NO consistency in those three. What can quantum physics create with conflicting messages. Energy might go take a nap or look for someone that has a consistent package to present while you pull yourself together and decide what YOU are all about today.

When your **actions** are hateful. Your **feelings** are wounded. And your **thoughts** are of love. What do you get from these three? And what would you suggest this person do to get real with themselves?

What exactly IS the message? Write it down someplace so when I ask again you will know the answer and be able to explain how your *acting, feeling* and *thinking* all support and strengthen each other. This is a test of your clarity of thought and action. Now if you do not pass this test you need to work on getting to know yourself better.

Maybe you could ask others what they see you as. Make a list and see if they see the same things. Do you agree with their observations of you? Humm.

So get clarity about WHO you are and what you are all ABOUT. Do that first so you can get your *acting, feeling* and *thinking* all on the same page.

IF you want to manifest CONSCIOUSLY and have credibility with the physics of the omniverse, create internally what you want to manifest externally. Be consistent, have integrity and honesty in your thought, feeling, and action. Do not try to control or limit your manifestation as quantum physics likes to handle the details and how your manifestation will happen on the third dimension.

Can you allow that?

Invisible realm likes handling the details because humans have a way of squeezing the life out of their creations as well as limiting their creations to death. Then sprinkle in all our doubts and it is amazing that creations get created at all.

OLD ENERGY: The old pattern was create anything you needed through thought and very hard work and forcing things to happen.

NEW ENERGY: The new template is that everything is perfect as it is and there is no effort or struggle needed. When you are vibrating high enough you don't need more pain and suffering. There is enough abundance and compassion available for everyone and all their creations.

YOU ARE **THE SOURCE** OF YOUR THOUGHTS.

Too many people focus on fear or what they do not want and what you focus on expands. Pondering on fear will certainly create more of that for you. When you put your faith in YOURSELF you reinforce your free will and your control of your life. The earth is ever-expanding good and we become participants in that flow. You are the one that shapes and controls your thoughts, feelings and actions.

The large majority of humans keep very busy to avoid an intimate close relationship with themselves. Humans give attention to the self in order to judge and criticize the self when they might well honor and have compassion for the self and all it has endured and triumphed over.

Developing an intimate close relationship with YOUR-SELF is easier to do during your alone time when you are in touch with the energy flowing around in your space. That way you can give yourself your full attention to the awakening process happening inside you. Get to know and increase your awareness about your shadow selves-the potentials you did not choose to explore this lifetime but were explored by other aspects of you. It is time to embrace all those options and aspects that carried out potentials you did not carry out. You collect and own all of those potentials into your oneness.

While spending quality time with yourself, check out your male and female aspects to see if they are in balance and ready to meld with each other. Unifying your polarities helps clear you of old habit patterns you might want to be free of, like negativity and fearfulness. Adjusting to your internal changes and rhythms allows you to integrate your unified self into higher frequencies.

When people repeat the SAME story over and over, they are probably STUCK in that story and might actually be asking a question, like why can't I get past this event? What can't I see? This story even bores me. They could be asking for help "seeing the bigger picture" so they can get themselves unstuck. You can be of great service by redirecting their focus within the context of the story they are stuck in. Come at the story with a fresh perspective and a much LARGER picture. Ask provocative questions like, "What lesson were you trying to master? Has someone given you this story and you feel they left out critical parts or twisted the meaning of events to meet their needs and possibly confuse you?"

Is an unfulfilling relationship consuming your time and energy preventing you from loving yourself? Selfishness is needed at this time. Giving more of you to others helps neither of you. Self -sacrifice is old energy. When the unspoken terms of your relationship mean you need to be less than you are, that is not serving you either. When the relationship with another or an organization means rules, regulations, or controls, you might be better off without that relationship.

Start owning how wonderful you are even without a spouse, job, boss or money. You are absolute PERFECTION. The person that needs your love is YOU!

The new energy is *safe*.

You do not have to worry about loosing control. You will not go out of control and start dancing in the traffic and drinking from the bird bath. But you could be liberated from limitation and what would your mom say about that!

So, are you CHOOSING to keep yourself small to uphold that self -deception and denial you were taught by everyone as you grew up? Or are you willing to have compassion and love for yourself? Can you embrace your divinity and dance on the roof tops with it?

ALL of us chose to serve in this colonization of earth and the new adventure into the world of matter. We gave up much to be here. We have all had to surrender our true form, our homeland and families, and become greatly limited. We even lost our freedoms and, with the veil of forgetfulness, felt separated from oneness. We chose the entire cycle of Earthly embodiments in the name of experience and increased spiritual wisdom.

Bonding with your invisible parts at this time and leaving duality is the completion of this journey we all signed up for back in the day. The spiral ride we have traveled on believing we were individualized consciousness separate and alone is ending. It is time for us to slip onto the new spiral of expansion with all our angelic buddies.

You can get your crayons out and draw yourself completing your journey and going to your angelic family reunion. Feel the emotion of the crayons you are using and the colors those feelings bring. Safety is warm and orange with clouds floating past. Excitement is pointed multicolored strips. Uncle John feels smooth or like a fuzzy speckled boxed in color. Sue is free to roam in green spots with yellow spaces. You see the rest.

Are you wanting to share the story that goes along with your drawing with a compassionate one? Then please do that.

As you become more interdimensional in your thinking and acting, know you have access to ALL your past life experiences. When you work with any of your past lives you ARE working with interdimensional energies. You can dip into your incarnations for talents, health, strength and awareness. All your past life attributes and characteristics are structured into parts of your DNA and available to you. Our past lives were us gaining wisdom and experience. Each incarnation brings a more advanced state that allows access to all we learned.

Free choice can keep us from accessing our past. We are afraid of the energy and power we have available and how we might have used it or twisted it. Maybe the people we know will turn against us and what we have to offer. So some go their entire lives without enlightenment, which is their choice to make, without any judgment at all.

Co-creation never included material things.

The things of co-creation are **peace**, HEALTH, *wisdom*, **happiness** and LONG LIFE and sustenance of needed items.

From a third-dimensional point of view, when we go to a past life to use an aspect of ourselves , we are reaching into the past and claiming THAT energy that is still active since interdimensionally it is "now" time and we are about to change our past and future by placing that energy upon our current life. We would be using the past to change the future along with altering the past by using energy that was only available then. The choice to bring forth the energy from a time past into our present.

The most interdimensional thing we have is our own DNA.

OLD ENERGY: the illusion of duality and separation is a close small picture. In duality, we are exposed to deceit, self-deception, corruption, greed, and decadence. It is confusing and challenging to maintain balance in the middle of these two opposing poles of energy. Karma is an old process in an old balance of energy system.

NEW ENERGY: is oneness and a much larger picture of compassion and the giving and receiving of unconditional love. A state of timeless serenity is present. In the new energy balance, the human has a support group made up of their past lives surrounding them with all the tools they will need to create mastery within herself and himself.

As we move into new energy releasing the old energy, we start to loose our emotional attachment to our history of this lifetime and all the others, for that matter. Anything we need to know or remember from the past will be there for us as we need it in the now moment. We move into a state of timeless serenity and wisdom when we pass 11:11 on December 31, 2011, it will end the Christos era along with the end of the Mayan and Egyptian calendar also. We will be moving into a spiral anchored in oneness and into the octaves or dimensions of seven through eleven opening up entirely new levels of awareness to us. We are moving from BEINGS having a spiritual experience to our SOUL having a human experience.

Are you being the creator working with ALL you have?

Are you relying on others to carry you? The New Energy is free and very abundant. Your job is to ACTIVATE the energy inside yourself. NO one else can activate your energy on your behalf.

***

A few can and HAVE made a change for the many on this planet AND will continue to do so. Less than one half of one percent of the humans could create a global shift and cause peace on Earth.

The principle is similar to when a law is passed that affects your life. No one consulted you or got your okay before things changed. A few people got together and agreed to create that change. Generally, it is the few that create change. We gave our power to representatives to make changes on our behalf that are best for the whole country.

What if the majority doesn't want what the few create? A rational answer takes a shift in your perception. The human is 10% of the whole. A large invisible part of our divine energy is in ongoing meetings with others around us all the time to create what looks like synchronicity. But it is well-planned based on our energy vibration and the direction our actions are going.

With the thinner veil comes a level of responsibility for the human to be in their passion with purpose and integrity. We are to step into our passion mistakes and all with joy in our heart knowing there is no right or wrong.

The flow of energy can never be hidden from empowered beings. Notice where the energy moves and follow the flow, energy never **lies**. You can see the intent of where the energy began and why.

All humanity depends upon the few who claim their mastery in spiritual awareness and divinity. They are the few that steer the planet's future and vibratory rate. *Intuitively,* they have been given permission to shape the future for the many. The rest of the humans may never wake up or become aware.

When Kryon was called in 1987 to move the magnetic grid of the earth, which in turn adjusted our DNA to the new energy, billions of humans had no idea it happened but at the DNA level, every cell knew. Magnetism is the largest force in the universe.

Magnetics is even more potent than chemistry in our univese.

Karma is an old process that was used in old energy to balance energy. In the new energy balance, the human has a support group made up of their past lives surrounding them with the tools they will need to create mastery within themselves. Former burdens of what karma might bring are now voided. Many are feeling this and feel disoriented.

Our DNA directly affects our aura and is the color of our interdimensional energy. We can only change our auric attributes by working with our DNA. Most humans don't believe they work with their DNA but they do. These are the interdimensional parts and are the ones that can be awakened into mastery by your own efforts. When we start moving in a particular direction our DNA adjusts itself also in that direction, making it ever so much easier to maintain the new behavior you wish to adopt.

For example:

Judging everyone and everything ran rampant in my family, and judgments were well-trained into me. When I was trying hard to release judgments of people and events in my life, I started having some success in releasing endless judgments but it was a real struggle. Then my DNA got shifted as a result of my movement away from judging and it was so much easier to greatly decrease the judging that ran around in my head.

Our DNA absorbs our energy of action in a particular direction and our 90%er helps us by adjusting the DNA . When the DNA adjusts, then your aura changes. So if you can see auras, you can actually see the change.

The human is in control of the percentage of dark and light they want to function in. Now is the time to take responsibility in either direction or any place in-between that you want to function in. When we choose to discover, embrace and meld with our divinity, we move into a sacred space of the soul taking the lead and the human being absorbed into the soul. As you work with your DNA you subtract a proportional amount of your third dimensional self.

You put yourself in kind of suspended state of being here, trapped in a physical body in a very slowed down energy so you could go back through and understand many of the things that happened when you were in the angelic realms, develop empathy and compassion to deal with the issues that your celestial family is having presently. It is the culmination of hundreds or sometimes thousands of lifetimes here on Earth, to learn those things about energy and about understanding yourself as a sovereign Being, so you could then work as a teacher with those who are from your angelic family. And that brought up many issues because some of you are wondering if you're ready.

Most of your energy has been focused within yourself, on the consciousness shift that we have been making. Everything comes to you for a reason. So listen carefully, scan and feel all energies. That's when the teaching starts with your listening and watching facial expressions, the body, eye movement and all that is NOT said. Observe their energy. Ask why they feel that way feeling their heart, divinity to divinity.

It is not wise to give the answer or solve their problems. Help them discover their own answers. Be steady for them when their life is in turmoil and they are lost in their own illusion. The words you use are not that important. Be a balanced and integrated energy example.

Find happiness within.

The feeling of loneliness might be persistent because you feel energies from family and friends. The gift in this loneliness is that you're learning to become a sovereign Being. After becoming sovereign, when you make the choice to be a part of something again, other energies cannot feed off of you and you're not feeding off of them. Once you make a choice it change the energetic characteristics of what is attracted to you.

That in itself now begins to bring in new and different opportunities.

You take in a deep breath to initiate your feelings and sensory energies.

Don't be afraid to work with your knowingness you can't go wrong with it. Your knowingness is part of you. It doesn't have a negative and a positive attribute because it is not part of duality. Your knowingness is the *simplifier, the problem solver.*

Energy is just out there, in a generally neutral state and it can be activated by your desire, passion, need or fear. Energy that has been activated by individuals or groups at some point can be released from them, and it just goes back into its neutral state after a certain evolution or time progression. Other energies are activated and never released but rather put out into mass consciousness. Sometimes when these energies are not tended to they tend to go into a state of confusion.

Even when you make a wrong decision there is a momentum going that will shift you into what is the appropriate balance for you. It is your 90%er doing this.

Change your perspective and look from the top side, you'll see a very beautiful weaving. Your creations are brought to life through this process we call the progression of a soul desire. A soul that has no needs or wants. The soul just wants to express and create.

Every soul has desire.

***

Tug-of-war with the brain

The mind wants to take over and interpret and analyze what is happening to the human all the time. The brain wants to TELL US what we SHOULD be feeling. Our mind and body have separate operating systems. The mind can manually override the body. WE ARE LIMITED BY BELIEFS WE DON'T EVEN KNOW WE HAVE. It is time to correct old tapes in our heads before we can change our behavior and direction. This is why we need to be clear about what it is we are feeling and what our thought are.

Feeling is about sensory perception, *not what the mind thinks* you should believe. We have sensory perceptions all the time. Things like feeling hot or cold, your clothes are too tight, you can't breathe or you are hungry.

The feeling has NOW moved from your sensory perception to thought and the mind puts itself in charge. Move forward with your feelings without trying to define them. This takes some practice to avoid defaulting to the brain. Work on experiencing the energies of your sensory perception and avoid the brain.

As we meld with our soul thought gets replaced with knowingness or your divine intelligence. The knowingness is not coming from you, it comes from your soul. The feeling is what we have DISCOVERED as an awareness from our soul. That is one way the soul communicates with the human.

Internal battles we have are imbalances of our intellect with our spiritual awareness, or the human 10%er trying to override the soul, the 90%er. Release those things that the intellect cherishes like self-pity, criticism, and "It's not fair." Claim your peace and serenity from the cosmic flow, through your 90%er.

Possibly you need to consult your "inner child" more. Your inner child can facilitates the connection to your soul.

As you move from brain controlled human to your divinity and universal intelligence, your 90%er will give you a POKE before your intellect can analyze your intuition away or negate it.

One of our missions was to transmute matter from a lower level to a higher level of existence. This necessitates a physical body from the third dimension to pass a gateway which only the higher energy can pass through. For this transmutation of matter to be accomplished, it needed to be done by a consciousness that had forgotten who it was-that had forgotten its eternal Being-ness and vast presence as angels within the body of God.

That consciousness would be humans and yes we volunteered. I don't have the memo either. The unseen world is NOT too big on written communication.

We are surrounded by other humans we do not FEEL connected to. Separation was also a requirement of duality. The two are inextricably intertwined, the marriage of spirit and matter, the transmutation of the human body into a higher vibration and frequency of energy. Our biological and auric processes are speeding up physically, emotionally, mentally and spiritually to consummate this marriage of human and their soul. We have been experiencing life from a higher spiritual perspective in bits and pieces. Until they all get in sync, we might experience anger and frustration. My personal favorite is impatience. I have lots of impatience along with the anger and frustration. You could say my cup runnith over.

What we have done on other dimensions is not impressive compared to giving earth life and us living in our creation. The things created on nonphysical dimensions are temporary and etheric. Imagination was used on the other dimensions and is used here when we start to conceive ideas and plans for building a thing or concept in the third dimension on earth. Imagination is satisfying but not full of life the way the third dimension is here on Earth.

Release the brain's concept of God.

The brain is WAY TO LIMITED to understand God.

She is unconditional love and compassion. The brain cannot relate to that. God has a presence within you and all around you. You are God also in a different way than the God of Home, "All That Is." Soul has always had honor for EVERYthing we are and do because EVERYTHING we do is sacred.

Soul and "All That Is" knows what it knows about itself through our human experience. God has wrapped us in total compassion for any experience we had and are having.

Changes externally and internally are happening to everyone on Earth as their 90%er deems them ready and starts to facilitate the levels and layers of change we are or will experience.

God is ALWAYS creating.

Creating is an expression of love.

We are creators and are being asked to be CONSCIOUS creators.

Back to your brain-remember it only knows what the human body knows. It was designed to care for the body. The mind DOES NOT go interdimensional. Angels without bodies do not have or need a brain.

You are not the victim of your life.

You have been the UNCONSCIOUS creator of your life. You were experiencing victimhood for God and she understands now. She "GETS IT."

Our ability to experience makes us VERY unique so we go through a period of emptying old passions from ourselves. And you feel as you might now, somewhat disillusioned, somewhat empty. But as you take a simple deep breath, that helps clear things up literally. Do not try to replace your emptiness with new beliefs or any new limitations. Breathe and allow yourself to feel life. No judgments, agendas or actions.

Releasing the old makes space to allow the new to come in.

Release experiencing to bring in creating.

The soul picks the time and place and you go along or you fight it. Your own divine self will shut you down when it wants a closer connection and some quiet time with you. We go into voids or a spiritual depression at those times so soul can get very close. You might not notice your soul because you will be wrapped so closely in your soul's compassion, you can't tell where you end and soul starts.

While in the void or a spiritual depression, you are FEEL-ING and actually are even more separated from loved ones, friends, family, and people in general than you have been. You may even find the lot of them in your way or very irritating to interact with. Coming out of the void, your energy will be transmuted into a very deep empathy and compassion for others and yourself. Your DNA will alter again little by little as you change it.

As you let go of Old energy ties, you might feel disorienta-tion, have a loss of memory or not be able to be highly focused. Those skills will come back to you differently when you are grounded in your new vibration. The old skills come back in a new way.

We are moving **from cycles** into a FLOW OF ENERGY and higher vibration. No need for a downside to balance out good things that happen to you.

You become aware of things you never saw before or ex-perienced before or have feelings we didn't know we had. That would be a result of all the aspects of you that you embraced and melded with.

WITH NEW AWARENESS, you will start another round of expanding yourself into other dimensions. We own the new information about ourselves, then we PROCESS the new information. When we put the new information together with our old information, there are many aha's.

Historically, when you experienced any emotionally trauma and you wanted resolution or peace about it you could be in for some long, drawn-out therapy for you to heal wounds or release stuck energy. With the new energy and your 90%er's cooperation, the long process of trying to remember all that happened and adjusting to the truth can be GREATLY shortened.

In my experience, there is no need to reexperience all the specific incidents and work through all the intense emotions. Key or pivotal events can be explored with the emotional charge experienced, owned and released with the invisible realm's help and understanding.

The unseen world wants you to feel and own those dense pockets of emotion stuck in your body and aura, all the painful and wounding events in your life. But there is no need to dwell there. Their interest is that you gather the wisdom and compassion for yourself and your experience and release those trapped pockets of emotions. I speak at length about this process in my earlier books.

The next step in expanding your identity is the INTE-GRATION of your divine and human self. That IS the big project, the overview that is underway-the process of bringing our divine self to our conscious awareness-THE LIFTING OF OUR PERSONAL VEIL.

Expanding one's identity wider and wider through the release of old pockets of emotional wounds stuck in your body makes you lighter. With new awareness and integration of new information comes new freedom and expansion.

Because we have bodies we can be conscious of ourselves. The Omniverse wants to be conscious of itself and will learn that consciousness through the humans.

Be in joy because whatever humans have picked to experience is the path they are on. We have free will. Being in joy and celebration no matter how bleak things appear. Celebrate your ability to choose and if you can't do that, you are not allowing yourself to be God also.

You have been the UNCONSCIOUS creator of your life.

***

CHAPTER 2

CHAOS THEORY

New Energy can be considered chaotic because we do not understand much about how it works yet. Judging the NEW with *old energy standards* of how energy functions is not helping us to clarify the way it functions. There appears to be disorder but the chaos theory is about finding the **underlying order**, in apparently, what looks like random data.

Historically, the philosophy and logic we have used to make sense of a very ILLOGICAL and *chaotic* world, has had limited usefulness and never did solve the problems of our world OR the people's problems on this planet. Something needed to change so the energy, stepped up to the plate, and changed.

The New Energy is present and affecting us and outcomes RIGHT NOW. New energy is in an inert state until your DESIRE activates it. The results we get with the new energy are unpredictable after a certain point. The energy works with your wishes but CANNOT be **controlled** or *forced* or CONTAINED. New energy is *very expansive* and moves in and out of all the different dimensions.

Our consciousness has not yet learned to follow the shifting and moving in and out. Everything is changing on multiple levels at the same time. Yes, that feels very chaotic to me.

We can no longer feel confident that future events will be linear, that illusion is slipping away on us humans. Cause and effects are happening on many, many different levels or dimensions at the same time and WHAT happens depends on which outcome you are focused on. The outcome would appear to be unpredictable using third dimension logic. Until you are able to expand your own consciousness to perceive many different outcomes on many different dimensions happening all at the same time you will see chaos.

Move to the much larger picture and discover the beauty of the synchronicity all happening at once. Experience the joy and simplicity of you observing many different creations going on in many different directions all at the same time, sort of like a kaleidoscopic.

OLD ENERGY: What we were taught in school. Energy is linear, if you do A and B you always get C no matter what the bias of the experimenter is.

NEW ENERGY: Is nonlinear and when you lack understanding of the way it operates it appears chaotic because it takes into consideration YOUR desires BUT cannot be controlled or force or contained. It is expansive and moves in and out of dimensions. Up to a point you can literally plot it and chart it mathematically .

✱✱✱

History of Chaos theory

The first discoverer of chaos could be considered "Jacques Hadamard," who in 1898 published an influential study of the chaotic motion of a free particles gliding frictionlessly on a surface of constant negative curvature. "Hadamard's billiards," Hadamard was able to show that all trajectories are unstable, in that all particle trajectories diverge exponentially from one another, with a positive "Lyapunov exponent."

Much of the early theories of chaos were developed almost entirely by mathematicians.

In the early 1900s "Henri Poincaré," while studying the three-body problem found that there can be orbits which are nonperiodic, and yet not forever increasing or approaching a fixed point.

Chaos theory progressed more rapidly after mid-century, when it first became evident for some scientists that "linear theory," the prevailing system theory at that time, simply could not explain the observed behavior of certain experiments like that of the "logistic map."

The ability to develop the chaos theory further was a result of the electronic computer. Much of the mathematics of chaos theory involves the repeated iteration of simple mathematical formulas. Electronic computers made these repeated calculations practical. When the computer rounded variables off to 6-digit numbers. The difference is tiny and one would assume it had practically no effect. However "Lorenz" had discovered that SMALL changes in initial conditions PRODUCED LARGE changes in the long-term outcome.

This effect came to be known as the butterfly effect. The amount of difference in the starting points of the two curves is so small that it is comparable to a butterfly flapping its wings. The flapping of a single butterfly's wing today produces a TINY change in the state of the atmosphere. Over a period of time what the atmosphere actually does diverges from what it WOULD have done. So the tiny change in a month's time could move or disperse a tornado that would have devastated a coastal city. Or maybe a devastation that wasn't going to happen does.

The chaos exhibited by an analog computer is truly a natural phenomenon in contrast with those discovered by a digital computer. "Ueda's" supervising professor, "Hayashi," did not believe in chaos throughout his life, and thus he prohibited Ueda from publishing his findings until 1970.

When we deny somethings existence, it does not prove it does not exist. It merely demonstrates how fear limits a person. Another case of denial failing to make reality go away.

The term chaos as used in mathematics was coined by the applied mathematician "James A. Yorke." The availability of cheaper, more powerful computers broadens the applicability of chaos theory. Currently, chaos theory continues to be a very active area of research.

In the book, A NEW KIND OF SCIENCE by Stephen Wolfram 2002, www.wolframscience.com

Wolfram says The Principle of Computational Equivalence: that when ever one sees behavior that is not obviously simple—in essentially any system—it can be thought of as corresponding to a computation of equivalent sophistication. This principle implies when it comes to computation—or intelligence—we are in the end no more sophisticated than all sorts of simple programs, and all sorts of systems in nature.

Programs based on simple rules do not always produce simple behavior.

When gravity is present, objects in general move on geodesic, curved paths. Geodesic is the shortest path. If space has appropriate curvature, one can get all sorts of paths. NODE, a point at which a curve crosses itself. Nodes are all proportional to the Ricci scalar curvature by a geodesic line or curved space.

✳✳✳

What exactly is chaos

According to Hesiod's Theogonia (The origin of the Gods), Chaos was the nothingness out of which the first objects of existence appeared. These first beings, described as children of Chaos alone, were Gaia (the Earth), Tartarus (the Underworld), Nyx (the darkness of the night), and Erebus (the darkness of the Underworld). Thus at the very start of his story Hesiod establishes the deities related to each element known to man beginning with the primordial elements: the Earth, the starry Sky and the Sea.

Theogonia presents two ways to come to life: division (Gaia, Nyx) and mating. After Gaia, almost all deities brought to life by division are negative concepts (Death, Distress, Sarcasm, Deception, and so on) and for the most part are produced by the goddess Nyx.

In Greek mythology, Chaos or Khaos is the primeval state of existence from which the first gods appeared from the dark void of space. In ancient Greek ['kha.?s] means "gaping void", from the verb, to be wide open. "In English" chasm and "yawn", Old English geanian = "to gape". Ovid, in his Metamorphoses described Chaos as a "rather a crude and undigested mass, a lifeless lump, unfashioned and unformed." From that, its meaning evolved into the modern familiar "complete disorder".

Chaos typically refers to unpredictability. The word did not mean "disorder" in classical period of ancient Greece. It meant "the primal emptiness or space." Due to people misunderstanding early Christian uses of the word, the meaning of the word changed to "disorder".

Mathematically speaking chaos means an aperiodic deterministic behavior, VERY sensitive to its initial conditions. An infinitesimal deviation of boundary creates a *chaotic dynamic sys-*

tem. The chaos theory is really about finding *the underlying order* in apparently random data.

Even though chaos is a mathematical phenomenon most of the research into chaos was done by people in other areas, such as meteorology and ecology. The field of chaos sprouted up as a hobby for scientists working on problems that maybe had something to do with it. Later, a scientist by the name of Feigenbaum was looking at bifurcation and how fast the bifurcation's come. He discovered that they come at a constant rate. He calculated it as 4.669. In other words, he discovered the exact scale at which it was self-similar. Make the diagram 4.669 times smaller, and it looks like the next region or section of bifurcation's. The scaling factor turned out to be exactly the same. He tried many other functions, and they all produced the same scaling factor, 4.669.

In math the concept of dimensionality only allows for whole numbers. Consider 4.669 a percent or fraction of a whole number. They are referred to as fractals. FRACTAL is a curve or geometric figure, each part of it has the same statistical character as the whole. A fractal is an object that has nonlinear characteristics and is self-similar at all size-scale levels. Self-similar in math, is an object or set of objects similar to itself at a different time or to a copy of itself on a different scale. An object with a dimension of 4.669 has a geometrical structure intermediate between a line, and a plane, which is three dimensional. The discovery of continuous dimensionality means that there are an infinite number of them that flow and swirl without limits or boundaries.

This was a revolutionary discovery. He had found that a whole class of mathematical functions behaved in the same, predictable way. This universality would help other scientists easily analyze chaotic equations. Now a simple equation could be used to predict the outcome of a more complex equation.

FOR EXAMPLE:

Blood vessels branching out further and further, like the branches of a tree, the internal structure of the lungs, graphs of stock market data, and many other real-world systems all have something in common: they are all self-similar.

By recording a dripping faucet and the periods of time between drips, scientists discovered that at a certain flow velocity, the dripping no longer occurred at even times. When they graphed the data further out they found that the dripping did indeed follow a pattern.

The human heart also has a chaotic pattern. The time between beats does not remain constant; it depends on how much activity a person is doing among other things. Under certain conditions the heartbeat can speed up. Under different conditions the heart beats erratically. It could be called a chaotic heartbeat. The analysis of a heartbeat can help medical researchers find ways to put an abnormal heartbeat back into a steady state instead of uncontrolled chaos.

DNA even though it holds an amazing amount of data could not hold all of the data necessary to determine where every cell of the human body goes. However, by using fractal formulas to control how the blood vessels branch out and the nerve fibers get created our DNA has more than enough information. It has even been speculated that the brain itself might be organized somehow according to the laws of chaos.

Computer art has become more realistic through the use of chaos and fractals. With a simple formula a computer can create a beautiful and realistic tree. Instead of following a regular pattern, the bark of a tree can be created according to a formula that almost, but not quite repeats itself.

Music can be created using fractals as well. (FRACTAL is a curve or geometric figure, each part of it has the same statistical character as the whole.)

Chaos has already had a lasting effect on science, yet there is much still left to be discovered. Aspects of chaos show up everywhere around the world from the currents of the ocean and the flow of blood through fractal blood vessels to the branches of trees and the effects of turbulence. Chaos has inescapably become part of modern science. As chaos changed from a little-known theory to *a full science of its own*, it has received widespread publicity.

Physics is no longer simply the study of subatomic particles in a billion-dollar particle accelerator.

PHYSICS has become the study of **chaotic** systems and how they work.

New energy is a CHAOTIC SYSTEM also.

Intelligence, wisdom, understanding and knowledge are **not** and never have been confined to just the brain. The heart, divine intuition is the true "seat" of knowledge and wisdom and the four attributes: intelligence, wisdom, understanding and knowledge are distributed throughout the entire body and across all levels of our soul.

Intelligence, wisdom, understanding and knowledge are part and parcel of the **very fabric of creation itself.** Think about that!

That would indicate that even a rock on the ground has within it an aspect of intelligence, wisdom, understanding and knowledge. That would be more than a mere spark of consciousness, right?

Somewhere along the line, the mind fought a dualistic battle with the rest of the body and declared itself the master of intelligence if not master of the omniverse. The time has come for this new consciousness to take its place as the seat of universal divine intelligence and give the mind a chance to rest up and reread its job description.

Energies are in a state of potential and sometimes what appears to be a state of chaos, because of OUR limited beliefs that prevent us from seeing various assorted potentials that lie in EVERY morsel of energy surrounding us in the moment. Present inside of us and NOW time, along with the energy in all of the other dimensions are at our disposal.

The convergence of all these energies happens on BOTH sides of the veil.

Setting one creation in motion produces a large number of potentials that were previously unknown BUT have always been there in a neutral state of readiness. They needed a CREATOR to set them in motion. This would be similar to typing a word in google and you get a thousand ways that word has been used. A thousand probabilities for the meaning or usage or location of that one word. When you have two different beliefs about a word and they interact you have created another larger set of probabilities.

All the probabilities are fascinating because there is just so much more than we have ever dreamed about. A small alteration in the initial conditions can lead to substantial divergence in outcomes. Chaotic systems in a sense are powerful vortical generators of New Energy and information! We only need to set things in motion and the energy (universal intelligence) creates a host of potentials. Anyone of the potentials you might pick will create more potentials in so many other directions we never anticipated.

So, structured chaos? A convergence of energies or just chaos?

***

Quantum physics

The "quantum leap" is for those that allow it in their life. Denial will work for a short bit maybe. On or around September, 18th, 2007, through 2012, things will not change at once. What will happen is that a whole new set of potentials or options will become available for humans to experience. The slow path of enlightenment or evolution will happen more rapidly than anyone ever thought it was possible to happen.

Physics is the study of the structure of consciousness. Quantum mechanics is more involved with probabilities pertaining to the subatomic realm. The study of the motion of quantities.

Quantum mechanics tells us its not possible to observe reality without changing it.

***

There is no such thing as objectivity or being an OBJECTIVE OBSERVER. We mistakenly believe that when we view something happening outside our body we are not affecting it with our thoughts and beliefs. THAT IS NOT TRUE. When our inner situation is not made conscious to us we believe what happens outside our body is a higher powers' doing or fate.

In **reality** we ARE creating the events around us.

Quantum mechanics views subatomic particles as having "*tendencies* to exist or happen." At the subatomic level mass and energy change unceasingly into each other. Quantum mechanics concerns itself only with **group behavior,** it intentionally leaves vague the relationship between group and individual events because they can't be determined accurately.

Newton says—you can picture it and he describes individual things and predicts events.

Quantum mechanics says—you cannot picture it and describes statistical behavior systems and predicts probabilities.

In the book, THE DANCING WU LI MASTERS by **gary zukav** 1979, Gary says, that new physics tells us that an observer CANNOT observe without altering what she sees. The distinction between the *"in here"* and the **"out there"** is an ILLUSION. Access to the physical world is a THROUGH experience. The common denominator of all experience isn't external reality, but ONLY our reaction to it.

Light behaves like *waves* or like **particles** depending on the experiment we performed. It appears that light has no properties independent of us. That's half of it the other half is without light or anything else to interact with we do not exist.

Properties belong to INTERACTIONS not independently existing THINGS.

Its not possible for us actually to see the geometry of the space-time continuum because our sensory experience is limited to the THIRD DIMENSION so its not possible for us to picture it.

The subatomic world is a continual dance of creation and annihilation of mass changing to energy and back to mass. The rules of classical logic are well defined and simple but don't correspond to experience. This and that are different forms of the same thing. If we substitute "subatomic particles" for people we have a good approximation of the conceptual dynamics of particle physics.

Quantum physics, at this time is mostly the physics of the incredibly small. While Newtonian physics can suitably describe the energy transformations during a game of pool quantum physics describes how the electrons surrounding the nucleus of the atom and other subatomic actions are interacting.

You may be thinking there is not such a big difference between these two sciences. The difference is that the applying common laws of physics begin to deteriorate on a smaller scale. For example, Nippendenso (Japan Electric) built a car that's only half a millimeters long. One could easily mistake it for a grain of rice if not for its gold color. At the scale of I to 1000, physics is already changing. Oil would now gum up the engine, and the tires wouldn't have enough traction to move the car.

Quantum physics tries to explain the behavior of even smaller particles like electrons, protons, and neutrons. Quantum physics even describes the particles which make up these particles!

The stuff taught in high school is no longer the prevailing theory. The electrons do NOT orbit like planets they form *BLURRY clouds* of PROBABILITIES around the nucleus. Protons and neutrons are each made of three quarks, each having their own IDENTITY and one of three "colors". Let us not forget the gluons that are even smaller particles that hold this mess together when they collect and form glueballs. Not a very scientific word but looks like the word sounds.

The quantum model of the atom is more complex than the traditional model which is why most teachers save that for college because it needs complex math to explain the behaviors and properties of the small particles. Subatomic particles are filled with quantum probabilities and ORGANIZED **chaos.**

Quantum physics TRIES to give us the statistical probability of the electron's location at any one moment. Scientists feel understanding the subatomic particles will lead to understanding the matter of the universe.

The comparatively new scientific areas of system theory and information theory have been around for the last forty years.

The theoretic microscopic objects physicists call STRINGS, postulates as the smallest bits of matter have as many as **10 to 26 dimensions** depending on which string theory one subscribes to. So far most of these dimensions beyond four are not observable because they are folded up somehow like a ball of twine into the other four dimensions.

Probably glueballs, I bet.

In the Super String Theory; Dimensions, length, width, depth and time are factors in the forth dimension. Beyond the fourth dimension things go 1,2,3,4, and ALL THE REST of the dimensions **at once**. Science is accepting up to the thirteenth dimension at this time.

Everything is in a quantum state all the time.

In the book *FUZZY THINKING* by Bart Kosko 1993 says Fuzzy rules are patches, you tie patches to data clusters. With enough data the fuzzy system can learn any system. Patches create nets. Nets are adaptive vector quantizes or AVQ nets. Data in rules out. AVQ points spread out to track data. You can use fuzzy nets to model events in politics, history, medicine, and military planning. Sets and fuzzy sets can model the many views in the debate.

Fuzzy thinking demands that you increase your options and use your imagination more actively than usual. Fuzzy thinking comes from fuzzy math sets in which endless possibilities have been explored.

Information preexists and is everywhere and is equally present throughout the matrix. Since information never goes anywhere you access it or it access you through the web's threaded network.

Move into chaotic disharmony until through pathways newly formed, coherence results.

We do not "LEARN" we **remember.**

We do not "**become**" we ARE.

Enlightenment is an on going process and not a plateau. Differing levels of heaven and hell are but stages of consciousness one achieves in the *Grand Spiral of Remembrance.* We reinhabit these thought forms in an effort to cleanse ourselves as we prepare for the next octave of growth.

We are **one mind** with *many thinkers.*

The ability to invent and create new changes for humanity as a whole will make a quantum leap in the new energy.

Chaos brings opportunity.

OMNI- PHYSICS all the potentials and their behaviors. Envision the potentials as bubbles that exist outside of physical reality waiting to be brought into physical reality. Each bubble on its own, representing a different potential. As the human brings things into reality the literal bubbles of potential gather together, as atoms do in all the molecules of our scientific structures. They are attracted to what you are choosing in your life and begin to come in. Sometimes they cluster all around you in a state of potential waiting for expression, reality turning into matter, opportunity or concept finding their way to you.

***

Ignoring astral evidence in the pursuit of scientific solutions is to decide not to seek the whole truth. When light is synchronous we are able to see it with our eyes. When light is asynchronous the waves align in a manner that makes us unable to see some matter.

Galactic math and math of spirit is ALL IN BASE **twelve**. The math of the universe is geometric math. It has to do with shapes and the energy around shapes.

Everything to do with the earth works in base twelve.

You have a choice of where your point of perception will be. For example:

When you receive bad news you might well want to ignore it. Say the news means you have lost all, your home family and vehicle and who you thought you were. You could go into a depressive state. Another way to see YOUR GIFT or perceive your bad news is that "everything is gone now" and you have no attachments any longer. Now you have all the new probabilities available to you. You could also laugh and in that laughter as you breathe in between laughs, you breathe in all the possibilities.

✳✳✳

Reality and Dimensions and Time

Dimensions are all related to each other and contain elements of each other. A dimension is relative to the thing they are describing. DIMENSIONS are growing in our awareness and in importance if you want to travel. Right we travel in space by going into one dimension and out another. Or traveling in *time* and SPACE is just a matter of changing dimensions. Energy moves and flows in and out of different dimensions. Your imagination can MOVE into and *through* all the DIMENSIONS. We solve challenges going through the dimensions.

DIMENSIONS are only consciousness and DO NOT occupy any time OR ANY space. You can create as many dimensions as you like there is "No limit." They are also exceedingly flexible. Dimensions overlay and intersect each other not on a mental level, this happens on a KNOWINGNESS level.

The concept of dimensions in physics relates to independent characteristics or qualities of something. For example a three-dimensional object has breadth, depth and height. Space and time in itself has four dimensional aspects.

Dimensions are a *FLOW of moving energy* not levels like many humans have been led to believe they are. Scientists say there are at least eleven dimensions in the heart of atomic structure. They are wrong because they forgot to count zero as a dimension.

As we start to sense other dimensions, we might feel a gentle confusion or "fuzziness" **of the senses**, as we begin to catch glimpses and snippets of all the other dimensions around us. A flow or a swirl of energy, dimensions don't necessarily know limits or boundaries unless they have been structured that way by the human belief system or some other consciousness.

We are living in a fourth dimension having height, width, depth and time. Each is a concept you can't easily make sense of unless you describe them relative to something they effect. You are short or tall in relationship to what or who? You are faster than what, and how much faster.

The aspects we "**tune into**" is what changes our reality.

There is a "circle of energy" that operates and affects this planet. When we move out of the third dimension into other dimensions, for instance when we solve problems or do certain spiritual things we become interdimensional in the process. When we connect with our soul and discover our divinity inter dimensionally, energy is released. The energy goes into the grid and the earth changing the fabric of what is possible.

REALITY is about **solutions**.

What have you solved or discovered lately? What spiritual interdimensional things have been grasped and incorporated into your life.

From a third dimensional point of view, when we go to a pastlife to use an aspect of ourselves we are REACHING into the past and claiming energy that is still active since interdimensionally is "now" time and we are about to change our past and future by placing it upon our current life. We would be using the past to change the future along with altering the past by using energy that was only available then. We made the choice to bring forth the energy from a time past into our present life.

We can also do the reverse, take energy from this lifetime and alter all the pastlives by resolving a conflict that was present in all those past lifetimes. In our past lives we often came in with the same issue over and over again.

For example:

For forty lives with the same individual Mary allowed her energy to be taken and used by Fred. This current life she refused anyone especially Fred to take her light and that changed all her relationships in all forty lifetimes.

Another example:

Richard had varying relationships with Elaine for twenty seven lives. He was never able to own his feelings of love and caring. But this lifetime he did own his feelings so that changed all the pastlives also to him owning his feelings.

**

The most interdimensional thing we have is our own DNA.

When you are working with your past lives in any form you are working with interdimensional energies.

Our DNA loops carry our contracts and Karma past and present.

Magnetism imprints us at birth along with our astrology.

Magnetism is interdimensional and part of our cellular structure.

Magnetics is an interdimensional force.

Magnetism is the largest force in the universe. Magnetics is even more potent than chemistry in our univese.

Our DNA has twelve loops, two are visible and ten are invisible. Our DNA has always been interdimensional. One the invisible ones are our karmic residue, life lessons, a print of what we used to be, spiritual contracts and the energy of the spiritual vows you took in past lives. Our astrological magnetic attributes, energy of our birth, day, hour, time and solar system. These are not in the forth dimension they are wrapped around gravity and time.

***

Now it is possible to step out of the life we are currently in and go into another dimension or lifetime, pick things up and come back to this one. As you exercise this skill you will pick up small items. You will pick up an idea or concept. Maybe you will pick up opportunities, possibilities, dreams, and thoughts. Over a short period of time you will actually pick up physical things from other dimensions because there is no stopping a human.

We can be in 2 places or more at the same time and one can affect the other.

We can never return to a less aware state its impossible for the human to unknown something. Some of us carry imprints of incredible sorrow and grief from past lives in a residual way, the feelings are still there. We're clearing them this time around

BUT there is no need to visit again what was actually experienced.

There can be potentials to clear out old structures or energies that have been suppressed, *hidden*, **buried** or rather distorted. New potentials can happen if you seek new options and manifest those options.

Drama vs a new potential which will you give YOUR time and attention. Which will you go with it is a choice thing. Potentials can happen that we never dreamed of there are whole new synchronicities available to us we never had before.

The new energy floods the earth and exists with the old energy. Time is literally speeding up this is an interdimensional phenomenon and is sensed rather than seen. To some it is felt in the biology.

Time is an illusion.

When you start *shifting dimensions* and having the experience of moving between dimensions, you will no longer have the desire to time travel because it will seem unimportant. Time is an illusion we have enjoyed during this illusion we live in. Time has nothing to do with anything else other than providing an opportunity to play a game in a linear timeframe with the illusion of past, present and future.

As we become comfortable traveling between dimensions we will make friendships in other dimensions of time and space. At times it is just a matter of closing your eyes. It is up to you the way you express this energy. You can bring it forward for your empowerment or for the use of others. Maybe use it for your own personal joy. The secret to humans becoming the highest person they can, on this planet, is through experiencing our own personal joy. Becoming multidimensional is one of the greatest uses of crystalline energy.

New energy can come in from another dimension and increases your **probabilities** immensely when there is a clash of beliefs between individuals or groups or countries. Even when you the individual are holding two opposing beliefs you could ball each belief up and imagine them colliding then observe the pile of probabilities that show up.

With the collision of beliefs comes the potential of new energy from ANOTHER dimension to come in and increase **probabilities**. These potentials are free to manifest for you personally, your creative project or business. The potential could even be for humans all around the earth.

New potentials can happen when you seek to manifest the options presented instead of getting caught up in the DRAMA of the clash of beliefs. Drama vs a new potential which will you give your attention? We have the freedom to explore new creative directions or keep doing what we always have done, getting the same old results we always got.

The new energy is UNPREDICTABLE and we *will not know outcomes* in advance. Outcomes are NOT PREDICTABLE. The shifting might appear chaotic but it is expansional. The "fine-tuning" of your connection to new frequencies and energies requires you to clear your body of baggage and blockages. Go within and listen to yourself. Your auric field information, is coming from a level your physical senses might not be perceiving yet. You start to feel energetic DRAIN from your physical body in the AURIC field when you are stressed by TIME, **energy** or *money*.

How well are you doing as part human and part divine walking between two very different realities. One reality we have very little experience with AND it is in transition.

Imagining, creating and manifesting will become the ENERGY of the future. Imagining, creating and manifesting will replace governments and religions and become the new businesses.

This is a new era with VERY dramatically new ways of functioning, using quantum physics and interdimensional math.

***

I AM means I am of the FAMILY of God.

I AM that I AM is a circle. You and I are eternal in all directions.

Honor your uncertainty.

WE do not need to prepare for the UNKNOWN. The entourage around us will do that. **Preparation is a virtue of old energy.**

KNOWLEDGE and PEACE about the UNKNOWN, with the ABILITY to DEAL with it are the virtues of the new era.

Blessed are the ascended Human Beings who understand the highest gifts we carry are *unconditional love*, **honesty**, INTEGRITY and holding your *spiritual light bright*.

Ascension status for Shaumbra and light workers isn't something we do, IT IS A WAY OF LIFE. Living in the NOW is living in a HIGHER vibration and that does not feel like it felt before when one was spiritual. As you solve problems duality will be pushed away and change its balance within you. Spirituality continues to feel different as a higher vibration continues to feel different.

Problems that the individual and humanity have had forever, will suddenly have answers and consensus in the new energy. Wisdom from spirit is being brought in. All situations are solvable with win-win solutions. When we can celebrate trauma, trial, hardship our inner light emanates from us and we become a catalyst for solution and change in our life. The solutions are found interdimensionally. Solutions we can't conceive of, our entourage can present to us. Will you receive them or follow and cling to your old patterns?

The inner CHILD within the human is least understood, it is the part connected closest to our soul. The child within has imagination and is responsible for the joy and humor found in the human. The child within is dependent and the adult or soul is present to contain the child in LOVE, **safety,** *protection* and structure. The adult or soul takes the child in and hugs and nourishes it. Its the child or human who accepts this and says "I need this structure". Its a marriage for life.

The child has INTUITION, **emotions,** *compassion* and WISDOM.

This angel never grows up it is always youthful, joyful, playful, laughing and smiling. This is the one that will create unity on this planet.

***

Questioning yourself dims your light.

Fear is generated because something is not seen or known like the future when we are linear. Once you fill that void with ANY truth, it is no longer possible to be in fear. That is fear, the opposite of love. NOW time is in a circle. When we stand in a circle of time we see the vastly bigger picture so there is no fear. Everything that ever was or ever will be is there in SOME FORM.

Humans living in NOW time have cleared their past life karma which is energy not completed. Now time is interdimensional, meaning you have blended the past, present and future potentials. Now time, leaves no room for past karma. If you should do something to create karma you will be forced to deal with it immediately in this lifetime.

The things we did are still in the now with us right now making up our reality. The future exists as "potentials of manifestations" in the NOW circle. As we manifest the potentials or not, the bias or direction of our reality box changes.

Is it real? What is reality?

All of what we see as history we believe to be an exact science, and yet time is much more flexible than we know. Invisible realm sends out a vibration of love energy that resonates within you if you so choose it. The vibration of love the invisible realm resonates in your heart center, enters your being and creates a third vibration within you that carries the truth. That is multidimensional and that is something that is starting to amplify.

WHEN we CHANGE we create a new reality.

The soul guides our invisible parts that go to meetings along with the human beings. We are all GIVEN THE ENERGY or challenge of new choices. Once you fill that void with any truth, it is no longer possible to be in fear.

We humans with bodies are part of the guide-sets of those we left in the last lifetime. We CAN BE in the past and the future at the **same time** in different timeframes. As long as we are human we will never understand it. As you read this you are doing something someplace else also.

The now circle belongs to the human because the human created it and can control it and be responsible for it. Reality isn't a thing or activity. Reality is about enabling yourself and having discernment and being a responsible creator.

To change one's reality you need to change your INNER understanding, your beliefs.

Although we participate in one reality we have *many to choose from.*

BUT only one at a time and it might not be the reality the people around you are in. Reality is variable. The lines that seem to be straight simply curve to meet themselves eventually. Therefor *time and reality are circular.* That is why things can be prophesied.

Potentials in a circle return constantly as items that have familiarity within the constant. The question is **how many times** will will you PASS a POTENTIAL on the circle before it becomes a reality?

Some things IMPLANTED in the **old reality** that were and *still are* for some:

—**Fear of enlightenment** was given to us so we constantly wondered what is real and what is not. The interdimensional layers of our DNA carries this seed fear.

—**Fear of abandonment** we want to fall in love with the other pieces of ourselves. Its a spiritual quest. When we marry ourselves on the interdimensional level we have calibrated ourselves. The piece that will never abandon you.

—**Fear of failure** is a *human setup* and voided with spiritual understanding.

—**Fear of self** that we might go into darkness and stay there.

—**Fear of darkness** which is passive. Light is ACTIVE and more powerful and a higher vibration than dark. *Secrets and conspiracy* don't remain long in the new energy.

—**Fear of other entities** or we fear what we don't understand.

—**Fear of not finding your path** it is *not straight,* so celebrate where you are.

—**Fear of disease** through human consciousness we can talk to cellular structure and renew and enhance, heal or clean it. Biologically we are made up of water as is disease and we can profoundly change water.

—**Fear of the future** the earth is going through awareness.

Our reality circle has changed and that's why prophesies are wrong. The NEW reality destination is one of **peace**. There will be a WISDOM **overlay** on *all doctrines and cultures.* Our new reality is giving us power over our own DNA and consciousness can change matter.

Truth *unexpressed* is not yet a truth.

TRUTH is not a single stationary object. When I spoke my truth people became fearful. They tried to find ways to negate my truth or put me down so they would not have to listen to my truth.

There is not ONE truth, real truth is *an evolution.* As we grow our truth changes. There are many, so many truths.

It is not important you speak the "perfect truth" only that the **truth is your own** and you are in **integrity** with what you say. Being in integrity with your truth is the only way that your truth can evolve.

Other people have their truths, and they thought my truth would interfere with theirs. Learning to live with truth is making room for truth around you because no one person holds all truth. Together you hold the larger blueprint of God. That is why each one comes in with a small piece. Find it and share it willingly not as the only truth, but as one that stands side by side with many others.

Real truth is only a perception and fleeting at best. It is not the expression of truth that counts, but the search for it. Truth is not the destination but the journey that is honored. Find your truth and express it in integrity. Do not worry if anyone understands it. Do not worry if you do not understand it, for you are being asked you to be in harmony and integrity with what your truth is. Actually speak your truth, stand in your truth and live in your truth so it can be reflected through the eyes of other people and you can see it yourself.

***

Time: Our past is only a memory.

In the past you are only as good as your memory tracks allow you to be.

Change that memory and you change who you are at this very moment.

There is a formula for **TIME** : The DENSITY of mass plus the rate at which it is VIBRATING = its time frame. There are varying *time frames* IN EACH DIMENSION and there is *circular time*. When you are in the now past and future exist together and meet in the middle. The now time frame is like a circle around us where all things past are known and future potentials are realized and known.

When the human SHIFTS their reality, the reality of time and our cells respond accordingly. Like rooms in a building we decide which reality we want to be in. Try not to use your brain too much move to your heart and feelings. Let the old ways of managing and controlling things, people and yourself slowly start to shift away from the mind making room for the new energy of the heart.

There are NO MANUALS for ascension or spiritual awareness but do keep it simple. Become aware of what is happening and then move forward, **watch and become aware** and move forward again. You need to be aware because the energy is *shifting and changing all the time* now.

You CANNOT predict the direction energy will move in.

Peace comes from realizing there is an overview and solutions are waiting.

NOW time and energy in interdimensional terms do not make much sense in the third dimension. For those of you moving to interdimensionalness I thought I would share some concepts of time with you.

Something that has happened to us and is in our past and is an event manifested. That event created feelings and wisdom that have affected our spiritual development in the present.

For example:

Being raised in an abusive family has made you wiser and more compassionate for others raised in abuse.

An event that was a probability but didn't happen but easily could have happened.

For example: Armageddon

When you realize what will happen if you continue on the path you are on you actively changed your path. When you changed your path, what you WERE doing is in the past.

For example: When you changed your path all the probabilities on the old path changed also.

After an event has happened and is completed you discovered a lesson you never saw before and you change your ways in present time.

For example: The same dispute that has always ended the same way, was altered because you changed YOUR reaction the last time the dispute happened.

It is very difficult for a human in FINITE form to understand the concept of infinity, as we are on the finite side of the veil even though our spirit is infinite. The invisible parts of us never end, never have a time out, never stops learning and gaining knowledge. Instead it moves from one energy form to another as it surfs throughout the universe in the evolutionary quest of soul.

If you tend to revisit the same question over and over, the now time circle is VERY small. When you go over and over something the energies laid down *previously are enhanced* and are more likely to **manifest**.

Stay in now time and take a deep breath in a quiet place. Allow yourself to connect with your own soul as if it were someone outside of yourself that you were meeting for the first time. Greet you soul and feel the love and trust between the two of you. Now focus your energy on THE GIFTS that you have received recently and ask your soul before you if you have received the intended gift.

Listen to the answer within.

Then you can begin to let go of it, blessing and thanking it for the wonderful role it has played in making you who you are this day. Returning to NOW awareness, allow yourself to walk forward with confidence. Even if you need to pretend the confidence at first, the soul confidence will build and offer you support that has never been there before. This is the first concrete steps in walking backwards in time.

Shifting dimensions of time and space is a most interesting concept but what can you do with it? The answers of the universe are not to be given to humans until they have formulated the questions. All the answers are deep within us. We have only to *remember our questions*. Formulate the question and we are able to understand the answer revealed to us.

The world is illusion, the first step to knowledge the wizard learns is not to trust her senses. The cycle of life and death continues on but only to the senses.

In the light there is eternal life.

Light energy is to be played with and shaped, that would be the joy of our existence.

Merlin was a title like the title teacher, doctor or scientist. There were many different individuals that were Merlin's and they were wizard's. The title carries a certain energy like all titles do. Wizard's go backwards through time. Walking backwards through time is a simple concept. First you **make the choice**. You plan to go out for pizza or become a scientist. Then you go backwards through time to see what it was like to get to your local pizza palace or become a scientist. This is an interesting dynamic that transcends time. We walk backwards in time all the time but we don't realize it.

FIRST you **decide** or *choose*.

In a way that choice has NOW been CREATED.

You structure the steps it will take to get there.

Get clothes on, get car keys and money to get pizza.

Take classes in math, science and spirituality to become a scientist.

A third option that will make you pretty nutty is to decide and *DO NOTHING*. So you live your life wondering why you aren't a scientist eating pizza—what is wrong with you? Where did you go wrong? Why do you feel like such a failure. Why aren't you doing scientific things and eating pizza? How can a mother love such a poor excuse for a human.

NOW you know the pitfalls of deciding or **creating** and NOT doing.

Are **YOU** possibly a human that never makes choices about where you are going to arrive so you **WANDER** in a timeless zone, wondering what you are doing and where you are going. The poor babies have been deprived of walking backwards through time. Their energy wanders around at night during their sleep. While the rest of us have places to go and angels to hang with.

Linear time has been artificially created for us to keep our awareness focused on the cause and effect of what we do and do not do. Events or points of separation on other dimensions have a circular pattern. "NOW" is the eternal form of time ever-flowing. Time ebbs and flows in the unseen world tied to how fast or slow awareness is happening.

Basically, there is no time. We artificially created time to help understand how to get from one moment to the next in our daily journey and understand cause and effect. Time is a belief system we divided energy into.

In other realms or dimensions, time is a **sequence of events** that takes place or *points of separation*. A series of choices or sequences that build one upon the other. If you want to grow flowers you would get seeds plant and water them. That sequence of behaviors produces flowers. The final choice to grow flowers has already been made. The sequence of events is just walking backwards through time.

Now you could have seeds from hard to grow flowers that will need much attention or care. Or you could decide to grow something like wild flowers. Low maintenance, you throw the seeds around and they tend to themselves pretty much, you do not need to water them.

When you are walking back through time this is NOT going back to past lives.

You had the experience because you CHOSE the potential.

Now you're experiencing how you got there in the first place.

Yes, it is possible to move forward and backward as well as sideways as infinite beings our true relationship to time is much different than we think. The first movement in time for most of us will be sideways. Moving sideways into other dimensional realities is as real and helpful as moving forward and backward in time. Both are becoming more possible than ever before. There are two ways you can work with this energy.

Are you aware that humans rewrite history every day?

If you do not believe that ask historians.

We are constantly evolving our stories of what has already happened. How many people in your family have rewritten the family history? We are the creators. We create everything around us in all the dimensions of time and space, by walking backward in time.

Therefore, WALKING BACKWARD in time actually means stepping intentionally into your future and taking your creator powers with you. In the illusion of linear time, understand that you are moving in one direction but facing another. So, walking backwards in time is actually moving into the future. Whenever you find yourself in any difficult situation you can move forward in time to see and create an outcome.

To walk backward in time in a linear time frame, you jump into the future.

Envision yourself sitting safely in your kitchen having a cup of coffee after working hard all day. Take a deep breath and feel what it is like sitting at the table after the event. Yes, it was (and is currently) exhausting, but you are okay now. You have just jumped forward in time. That is walking backward in time and that is practical magic.

Energy in front of you supports your creations.

Look at how things are going to feel when you say you have done it. Now what is important to me what is exciting to me? That is the creation trigger that puts things into motion. The possibilities are what activates the soul. Let yourself get excited about the possibilities.

As we walk forward in NOW time with a confidence in our soul we never had before, there are opportunities for us to go back in our own history and rewrite events. To rewrite events with a strong emotional charge on them that might get you stuck.

All events in your life have a purpose. There is *a gift in every event that crosses your path*. In order to rewrite history, you must first receive the gift. If you have not received the gift, you cannot change where you are in relationship to the time line.

So the first point is to find the value of the experience or circumstance that you wish to rewrite. NOW for the first time, we can actually rewrite the emotions and energy around our past events with an enlightened mind.

The abusive father was actually your partner in karma. He did an excellent job of stirring you up. Ah, that was the gift. The one that shamed the family, gave you a kick in the pants to help you become more spiritually aware. Another gift!

The partner laying next to you is becoming more precious to you with your new divine eyes. Another gift!

You are rearranging your memories and REWIRING your **brain.**

One foot in old and the other foot in the new energy. When you change the angle you view something, you also change the way it appears which changes YOUR REALITY.

Now more than ever, we are feeling the compression of time and space. Those things that used to bring great joy are somehow not as nice as they used to be. As we step into a higher vibration *we reach for higher truths*. Take a daily walk in the inter-dimensional bubble of love to feel peaceful and loved, that way your cells will be refreshed and refuse to go into drama, anger or worry.

Do not set goals as they are limiting.

Instead, plant the seed of how you will feel when you are planning your next stage of evolution. Understand that your infinite self or soul has REALIZED these goals the moment they are solid thought.

Emotions bridge the gap in the time line. The link between the finite and the infinite is the emotional energy we bring. The way we experience how it feels to design our next goal or project, that sets up the greatest of possibilities.

Linear time and now time, in a circle or balloon, **exist together**, one is an illusion.

The invisible realm no longer interferes with us by showing us "the way," for we are doing fine on our own. They shine a beautiful light on our path so we see a little more clearly.

Love does not exist in the same field as science.

Technology and physics follows consciousness when you are ready the new awareness will appear much faster than it ever has before. We will be using light to change water to create new energy sources.

Our world is made up of three's. The cosmos is based on a mathematical base system of twelve. But, this illusion of free choice is a fraction of that vibration based on three. All of our world and everything in it can be reduced to the number three and we call it the third dimension. Giggle, cosmic humor.

Now that range is expanding.

As we begin to experience other dimensions it will be helpful to have tools that help us cross from one dimensional level to the next. This is not new information as it has been known by many as far back as ancient Egypt. It was believed even then that the world was made up of three's and that the door between dimensions was accessed through a 90-degree turn.

New energy is in an inert state until your DESIRE to activate it.

The New Energy is present and affecting us and all our outcomes.

RIGHT NOW

***

CHAPTER 3

Energy EXCHANGE and BUSINESS

Any energy exchange continues to keep on exchanging and EXCHANGING AND exchanging some more. By the time the energy comes back to you it might not be immediately recognizable as something you sent out. The energy comes back in many different forms; as a new idea, a broader awareness, a grant or gift, or even new people or entities for your business, there could also of been good will for your company generated.

As the law of attraction says we get back more of what we put out. Probably a good reason to spread good will.

In economics, **business** is the social science of managing PEOPLE to organize and maintain collective productivity. **Business** works towards accomplishing particular creative and productive goals to usually generate a profit.

When you believe that all profit is a bad thing, you might put yourself into a belief system of lack. A belief system of lack can cause you abundance challenges for ever and ever and ever.

Being poor is not a lack of money it is a state of mind an energy where you believe in your own lack of creation and your own unfamiliarity with your creator abilities.

The singular usage of the word business refers to a particular company or corporation and the generalized usage refers to a particular market sector. Like "the computer business" or "the business community" consist of the community of suppliers of goods and services. The singular "business" can be recognized as a legal entity within an economically free society where individuals organize a group based on their expertise and skills to bring about social and technological advancement and services.

In predominantly capitalist economies businesses are typically formed to earn profit and grow the personal wealth of their owners and / or share holders. Notable exceptions to this rule include many cooperatives, nonprofit organizations and many government institutions.

Owners and operators of a business have as one of their main objectives the receipt or generation of a financial return in exchange for their work, time and energy and for their acceptance of risk investing work and money without certainty of success.

Most Marxists used "means of production" as a rough synonym for business. Socialists advocate either government, public or worker ownership of most sizable businesses. Some countries advocate a mixed economy of private and state-owned enterprises. Others advocate a capitalist economy where nearly all, enterprises are privately owned.

We have a CHOICE as to where we want to spend our money.

We can choose how to form our own corporations.

We want to become part of the solution instead part of the problem. The shift ahead does not need to be a difficult one. The shift IN ENERGY AND CONSCIOUSNESS does not need to be destructive. It can be from the heart and reflect a proactive mentality.

When a corporation puts the heart energy of the people first, they will actually make more money. The corporate bottom line will actually improve but very few businesses have proved that out yet. Many corporations are already starting to transition their vision into heart energy, so align yourself with those people and organizations.

Even as you form your own small businesses, put that energy into your business plan. "How can I be of service?" Support the corporations that put that into their business plan. Our new energy businesses will be the melding of the physical human in the third dimension working with and in cooperation with angelic, spiritual help from the unseen world.

Our skill at imagining, creating and manifesting will become the core energy of business.

All energy *moves* and EXPANDS and **rebalances** itself.

OLD ENERGY: Goes in one direction, to the bottom line. Business felt the end justified the means to increase profits. Each worker had an hourly wage tied to themselves. She is a nine dollar an hour, pink collar person. The equation too frequently is WIN—LOOSE.

NEW ENERGY: Goes in multiple directions which is beyond our current consciousness. The new energy business to succeed has to have consciousness and creative thought working hand in hand. The money shows up as a result of your creativity, compassion and honoring all those involved at all the different levels. The new energy business will be physical, spiritual, compassionate and creative all at the same time. A WIN-WIN-WIN-WIN-WIN proposition.

The new government and religion of the world will become the business of imagining, creating and manifesting.

Instead of creating an outcome we have asked our governments to create on our behalf for us. We gave government our power or energy. That way we held our government responsible for our creations. We have not been too impressed with what government has created for us.

In every region of the world governments have been created. Big ones or little governments, makes no difference they are all basically the same. It is human nature to want to make life easier and have many of life's necessities provided for us by an organization. The problems arise when we ask them to lead and create for us.

The majority of people have been controlled by those in political, religious and industrial power. The majority of these groups constantly send out opinions and propaganda to convince the masses they will solve everyone's problems and make their lives much better and safer. We have learned to follow the leader without question.

In reality it has been a way to take and keep control of the masses and siphon off as much energy as possible.

What would it be like for government to be returned to being the servant of the people rather than a servant of itself or those representing us. If humans are willing to take more and more of their own power back, the role of Government would *change and decrease.*

We need to demand that our government be VERY transparent and of service for the public good. We need to elect the people that will change things to allow corporations to use their heart energy. If a corporation is to be deemed a legal entity then make it illustrate that it has a heart and uses it. This is about using practical magic. Learning to honor the god within each one of us and become comfortable with our divinity.

Hold the concept of a transparent government working for the people's best interest in our heart first, for we have power unequaled throughout the universe. Each and every one of us chooses the reality in which we live. Or you choose a reality where you are your own person and you let government adapt to you. When someone pulls the rug out from under, that ripple goes through the entire carpet and shakes everything up. The ripple does not need to happen in a destructive manner, it can be a gentle change. It can happen one heart at a time.

***

SOME HISTORY for YOU and me

Historically, energy of all different sorts stayed WITHIN each countries boundaries as did the politics, government and religion. Energy didn't like the restriction much but accepted the limitations forced on it. Our consciousness was evolving VERY slowly. Humans stayed in their own small areas with the very smallest group, controlling and dictating what would and would not be done to and for the larger group of humans. Things went on and on like that because there was no energy strong enough or interested enough to alter the tight energy loops of exchange that went on in each country.

Maybe a hundred years back and way before that churches **were** THE *largest business of all* controlling more of the land, money and the mind, the heart and soul of its people. The churches used their theology to cement their controlling, limited, belief systems. A small group of the religious leaders, claimed WHAT God wanted for all the humans.

You DO know that is not what God said or wanted.

Boundaries of countries have become blurred because the business community wanted to increase their profits and by extending their business to new and different people or countries. Energy was in support of all of that because energy just LOVES to move IN and OUT and all around changing its many outfits and different movements.

For the past forty years or so business has been in the business of brokering how and when and where energy will be exchanged in and out of many different countries.

Business, is in the business of brokering deals between countries and individuals. Business in one country was brokering deals to do business with a company in another country. Business has negotiated with governments and religious groups to flow goods and services to and from individuals, companies and countries. Rules regulations and laws have been changed to accommodate these movements. Companies have replaced the energy movement that religions and the governments possessed at one time.

The personal greediness of the few money grubbers at the top has left a sour taste in our mouth for the way religions, governments and corporations have handled or squandered the money at their disposal. Most of us consider companies to be self serving and insensitive to the worker.

The upside, the gift, for those that did live through Enron and other companies of that ilk is that there deceptive practices have woke people up and demonstrated what NOT to do in business. The old energy practices of corruption and favoritism is being driven out and cleaned up. Gaia, with her winds and other energy redistribution's has been doing a lot of restructuring herself, the last few years. Gaia plans a few more years of disruption and redistribution and restructuring of corruption on earth.

There are no accidents.

Business is replacing and slowly becoming the **largest energy exchanger** present in politics, religion and governments. Have you been observing that change over? There might be a quiz. You aren't letting "the OTHERS" decide what is best for you are you? That is what we did with Enron.

Let us look at a few reasons WHY we might prefer business being the larger exchanger of energy instead of the "other groups". I know the "other groups" function just as business has historically. The few greedy ones at the top of the food chain get all the goodies and the "worker bee" gets to supply the goodies, just as things go down in any pyramid scheme.

A large difference between countries VS businesses exchanging energy is that businesses NEGOTIATE and countries tend to have wars, bombs and hand to hand combat type things which is dangerous to the body. How long do you need to decide which means of resolution you would prefer for you and your fellow humans at this time?

Negotiations are milder and gentler on the body and spirit than wars are, as we all well know except for the few we put in power that do not "get it" yet.

But than their agenda might be vastly different than yours or mine. They might have exactly what they want.

Another point about the corporate world unlike governments and religions is their high motivation for profits. When a company sees a highly successful business, they mimic what they see, that works. A company using consciousness at all levels of product development, distribution, handling of clients, customers or employees will be mimicked. That type of motivation is absent in religion or spirituality and definitely in government.

Business is an unending energy exchange in lieu of one country DOMINATING another countries energy. In the past there was a finite amount of energy now the supply of energy or money is almost endless.

Endless, *I tell you!*

A new bunch of energy has been slowly arriving, yes the winds of change are here to stay. You can choose to tag along or acclimate to the changes. Or, you can help direct the energy movement and exchange.

BUSINESS will be the new government and religion of the world.

Business will be negotiating the interrelationship between human beings and their countries.

The ability to **imagine**, to CREATE and *manifest* is the **core energy** of what business is all about.

Humans will also adapt a belief, and then they **will manifest** that belief. Most of the time we do that on the subconscious level. Occasionally we do manifest consciously. We create our own truth. When you think you are a powerless victim that is what you become over and over again.

We really are that grand and the master of our own energy.

We can create ANYTHING even the illusion that we are *just human.*

Anytime you restructure your beliefs or create new beliefs for yourself, it is like a factory. You put energy and beliefs in with a how to list and presto you have a consciousness factory. Parents and teachers and governments do it all the time. Our government put energy and fear into the factory. To protect us from this amorphous fear and we keep giving up our rights so we will be kept SAFE from a bureaucratic mess that cannot even help hurricane victims or "identity theft" victims.

I would rather do my own deciding about what is safe.

✿✿✿

Creating a business plan ought to be a piece of cake for us angels above and below. Before arriving on earth we created our own SPIRITUAL individual business plan for the thousands of years we have been hanging out here. Meeting, updating and renegotiating the original contracts all along the way. The over all plan for the group was to evolve spiritually in lieu of amassing piles of energy or gold.

In the new energy, spiritual and human businesses shall be surpassing all the old energy "businesses institutions" in power and their spiritual awareness.

WE HAVE PEOPLE, parts of ourselves and other entities of course!

Brilliant brainstorming sessions, maybe some not so brilliant are held all the time in the unseen world with our 90%er attending and participating. Then when agreements has been reached on a group of the most likely probabilities, the human has the option to pursue what she would like to create. Hopefully she has the determination and knowledge to bring the probability into the third dimension allowing it to manifest into our reality.

Now with our individual veils getting thinner and thinner it is becoming easier for the unseen world to get closer to us and be more hands on, helpful.

Add to that the new "fourth dimension meeting place" composed of higher vibrating entities, that will be more constructive and helpful than they have ever been before. The new energy businesses will have an edge OLD energy business never had before. The goal in business is INTEGRATION of our divine energy with our human energy the same goal we have for the individual, integration of the divine self with the human self.

Energy is ENERGY, right?

NOT only will a product or service be offered to people so will the "energy of potentials" be sent out with the product or service. How the receiver plans to use or NOT USE the energy is their choice.

A few thoughts about CASH.

We pretend that money in itself has value and it DOES NOT.

Money is only an object we all agreed to give a value or energy. Just as in your business and for those purchasing your product or service, the real exchange will be your energy to them and their energy back to your business. With the cash being a measure of the amount of energy being exchanged among humans. Energy will also be exchanged between the unseen world and the seen world.

The cash will come in naturally as a result of the raised consciousness. Any energy exchange continues to keep on exchanging and by the time it comes back to you it will be transmuted and transformed. Coming back in many different forms as a new idea or awareness. Your new energy business will be spiritual and fun the melding of a physical and spiritual energy or the human and the unseen world working in tandem.

Energy *moves*, EXPANDS and **rebalances** over and over again. Your business will be a new way to move energy.

Hoarding will be frowned on in the new energy. Piles of gold or any other hoarded commodity not being put in the flow or used, will get dispersed on the human by the unseen world. Leaving things just sitting around INCASE they will be needed or wanted at a very future date will not be tolerated well in the new energy business.

Now if you hung out with energy and conversed with it a while, I suspect it would tell you that it is not too fussy about the way it is used, BUT it strongly objects to NOT being used. Just sitting around waiting for long periods of time to be used makes energy get a bit cranky and out of sorts, not to mention unbalanced. The quantum physics of new energy will go into action and disperse whatever you have hoarded.

ENERGY loves to be *IN the FLOW it lives to* **MOVE**.

Energy loves to be transmuted and wear different outfits, to be bartered with and exchanged for new and different events, things and ideas. OH! Energy just loves to flow in and out and all around every place you allow it. Energy is not to keen on being told what to do. Just like humans. But it does need a push to get started, like a lot of humans.

Humans have spent gobs of time developing a very sophisticated and precise system of energy exchange that all businesses use and the angelic realm is fascinated with the preciseness of the exchange system humans have worked out. The angelic realm is looking for ways to play our "energy exchange game of money" with us, it looks like fun to them. They want to be dealt in. Money is the refined **science of energy exchange** and the way we as a group have agreed to let it make the world go round.

The bare bones of any business is an *energy EXCHANGE.*

Business is **NEGOTIATION** and then **exchange** for goods or services.

Time to live and experience without the *ILLUSION of safety.*

Time to choose what YOU desire rather than protecting your gold. Setting up a new business brings up old fears about all you LACK. Questions about attributes and yourself. Now if you try to cover your fears and questions with Pollyanna dust, you haven't addressed the different energies that came forth to work with you and support your endeavor. The fears and questions will keep trying to get your attention they are only energy with a job to do and want to help.

You are the one guiding and collecting information to pull this venture of exchange together.

There are FIVE main types of business units:

Sole Proprietorship: a business owned by one person. The owner may operate on their own or may employ others. The owner of the business has **total and unlimited** personal liability for the debts incurred by the business.

Partnership: A partnership is a form of business in which two or more people operate for the common goal of making profit. Each partner has total and unlimited personal liability of the debts incurred by the partnership.

Cooperative Business: or Co-Op a cooperative business structure: for-profit, limited liability, members of the co-op share decision-making authority. Co-Ops normally fall into three types: consumer co-ops, producer co-ops (common in agriculture) and worker-owned companies.

Private Limited Company (Ltd): a small to medium sized business that is often run by a family or the small group who own it. The owners and managers are only liable for the business up to the amount they have invested in the company, and are not liable for the debts incurred by the company unless they have signed a personal guarantee.

Public Limited Company: a business with limited liability, a wide spread of shareholders and in the UK, a share capital of over £50,000. The owners and managers are only liable for the business up to the amount they have invested in the company, and are not liable for the debts incurred by the company. In the United States and some other countries, a limited company is known as either a corporation or a limited liability company.

A TIME OUT please.

I want to address the group huddled in the corner whining!

The ones that are always saying YOU CAN'T DO THAT because **I am scared**. The people that REFUSE to take ANY responsibility for themselves. Workers that refuse to control their own energy so they give it away. They refuse responsibility for loving and honoring themselves. When you give away your energy you can blame "the others" for your misery and high level of fear.

The boss says it is "the workers fault" and the worker says "it is the bosses fault" for abusing us so. We have acted like trusting sheep never thinking for ourselves and the BOSS took advantage. A circular argument going no place—trapped cranky energy.

Most humans are like the farm animal staked to a pole moving in the same circle day in and day out. The concept of freedom is not even considered. They are locked into old systems and being told what to do and when and where to do it. Bah! Bah! Bah!

Haven't we enjoyed our victimhood enough all ready or maybe not.

We are still encouraging anyone willing to control our lives and take responsibility for us because we refuse to control our own existence. Some refuse responsibility for themselves at ever turn. Its the churches fault, the governments fault, the school boards fault and my mother-in-laws fault too. It could even be the dogs fault I am like this and if it was good enough for my parents and grandparents it is good enough for me!

The above is not a trailblazers point of view.

FOR THE GROUP LOCKED IN FEAR DEMAND-ING OTHERS BE RESPONSIBLE FOR THEM I know you enjoy that game so feel free to move to the next chapter do not bother with the rest of this one.

✷✷✷

FAILURE is Part of the PROCESS silly human.

Who has succeeded that didn't fail first?

We FAIL so we can look again at what we are doing and *EXPAND* what we are doing, *Allow failure*. Failure is your friend, remember when you had coffee and conversation with fear, failure and fun, the "F" triplets. You got pointers from fear, failure and fun, you asked for their support and wisdom.

Failure unravels stuck energy and smoothes out the rough spots.

Failure is a *teaching tool* and redirects the future of things that might not work as well as something new would. Being afraid of failure will stop or cripple your creation AND you get to join the ranks of the talkers that don't do.

That is a much bigger crowd.

Use the stumbling blocks of experience for receiving greater intelligence. Be free to stumble and you will learn great new things.

Maybe the quantum formula is fail and learn, + fail and learn, + fail and learn = expand your resources and your creation. Then succeed + succeed + succeed = a new or slightly different creation.

You do not need to go down the old worn paths, create many new paths.

It may also be difficult or impossible to ascertain whether a situation meets the criteria for failure or success due to the ambiguous or ill-defined definition of those criteria. Finding useful and effective criteria to judge the success or failure of a situation may itself be a significant task. However, it should be remembered that failure is the stepping stone to success.

A **commercial failure** is a product that does not reach expectations of success, failing to come even close. A major flop goes one step further and is recognized for its complete lack of success. Obviously, due to the subjective nature of "success" and "meeting expectations", there can be disagreement about what constitutes a "major flop."

It is absolutely one hundred percent Human nature to be impatient, and also to feel urgency when there really is none. When you get information about "taking the next step," why not immediately also *go into a "now" consciousness and "see"* the TIME LINE? Most Humans think that it means right NOW. Then they move toward energies which are simply potentials for the future. To make the situation worse, they don't get results, because it's not time yet. Then they say, "Well, I tried that and it didn't work."

How sad is that?

What you "feel" needs to be done right now, does not need to be done right now. There is time. Relax, and allow another three months or so to pass. Invisible realm is not in a hurry very often as you may have noticed.

For those humans that fall into the category of "tried it and failed," review what you have done and check your time line again. It takes a bit of work for humans, but do try to start getting in step with the timing of the unseen world.

Don't throw away anything that you tried! You might want to try it again. The times they are a changing. This is all part of the new quantum physics process.

Humans are needing to increase their insights and flow with the consciousness of the unseen world. We are not being cared for by the unseen world any longer. Scary as it is the humans are calling the shots AND the unseen world is *creating the time line*, linear or round. Round of course. The unseen world creates the synchronicity.

Humans need to know WHEN as well as *what*. The unseen world is making us pull our weight, no more fearful coasting!

Do not be afraid of WASTING TIME or resources on something that might give the appearance of failure, you HAVE gotten the wisdom and truth. The ACTION or intent of venturing out signals to your soul that you have **decided to move** into what you planned.

HAVE you gotten the wisdom and truth?

That is what is important. That is the WIN.

***

BUSINESS in the New Energy

An unending energy exchange, that is what business is. In the past there was a finite amount of energy now the supply of energy and money is almost endless. The increasing consciousness on earth, along with the new energy businesses that are springing up and are becoming global.

We are increasingly operating from the HEART and being compassionate to all that touch our businesses. The unseen world is being supportive by helping-forcing humanity to vibrate higher and in love.

An example:

When the animals we eat aren't being treated humanly we will start getting sick from eating that animal or those crops. The animal and crops need to be honored for their service to us. All that energy will balance itself OR when we do not "get it" the angelic realm and quantum physics will help us figure it all out! Getting sick, will help the slow learners, learn.

A new energy corporation is a **CREATIVE** POOL of energy **expressing** itself at times as a business. The workers and vendors, the management, buyers and sellers will need to focus on the heart energy to succeed. Focus on the heart will balance out the bottom line.

The country your business is located in is all part of the wholeness of your operation. All parts will carry aspects of the other parts. All you work with have an energy contribution and you contribute your energy to them. We all share energy to keep the business in the flow and the heart. The energy will flow to each in their appropriate proportion.

OLD ENERGY: Owners chose the bottom line as their priority not the work force. Energy movement was in one direction. Jobs are boring and limited. Workers were not honored.

NEW ENERGY: Create from the heart. Consciousness needs to be alive along with a creative pool of energy expressing itself in many directions. Spiritual consciousness is moving into business and all the people involved.

***

Stages to **CREATING** reviewed:

There are four stages to creating anything and that would apply to a business also. You start with, and at the core of everything, there is desire or passion. That desire is in our beingness and installed in the DNA so the unseen world knows all about it. Desire is NOT a want or need.

DESIRE or **passion** is hard-wired in.

You have the idea or feeling so how long have you been playing with it?

DESIRE or **passion** at play:

Check your timeline. If you have been playing with this desire for years or decades or even created it once and were not pleased with your results update what you have going on and run it through the new energy, you will get different results this time.

Play with its architecture, not in two dimension or three dimension. Put your passion in the fourth dimension and beyond. Feel the NEW math and NEW energy. Look at it and watch it go into itself and MOVE in all directions. The shape gets larger and smaller or fuzzier it might even have open spots, stripes or pokadots, just watch it flow.

BUILDING stage:

When you are ready move your business to the BUILDING stage feel your shapes, singularly and in groups. Feel the differences in their flow. Spend some time in the crystalline realms with your shape, or for ideas, or even your timeline. Numbers and shapes or pattern are changing their characteristics nothing is as it used to be. Stay general at this stage so you can see what wants to JOIN your project and what comes to work with you.

Decide on an aspect to develop and structure your business beyond two or third dimension, take it to the quantum level and the many dimensions. Build and feel your business, feel it small and larger, feel the flow difference. Go to the crystalline realms or the new fourth dimension with your concept. Patterns and shapes will change your creation. Nothing is as it used to be. Keep things simple so it is easy to morph into other ideas.

Putting your limits or doubts in the equation at this time will shut your project down for you. The project wants to please you and do as you, the creator want it it to do. Pleasing you the creator is EVERYTHING. It's the old saying, "Careful what you ask for you might get it."

ATTRACTING stage:

Time to ATTRACT potentials and other related energies, people and resources. Don't think it or force it, attract your probabilities by putting your vibrations out there and mingling your vibrations with others. Avoid getting all intellectual or detailed putting bows and ribbons on it because that will start to limit the vibrations you are sending out. And for heavens sake we all know you want to avoid limitations on your business.

New energy and your higher vibration makes creation so much faster than it ever has been before. Open up your consciousness and feel it. Be aware of the currents in and around you. Solutions and new ideas to consider come in faster and from so many different places in the new energy. Shapes, numbers, colors and symbols have an openness they NEVER had before. This is great for those that have very expansive concepts.

Our **reality** base is also changing.

BUILD the prototype calling on the basics feel the synchronicity come into play that is the invisible realm jumping in to help you out. The appropriate energy and resources are attracted to your project. Place no value or judgment or lack of money on the synchronistic stage. Keep the ideas wide open.

You feel everything went wrong?

That is the perfect time to start over! See what you get the second or twelfth time around. I repeat keep ideas WIDE open.

Sometimes ideas and concepts will get blown up or broken or morph into another direction. Not to worry you have just experienced fail and learn + fail and move stuck energy + fail and unravel new concepts = expand or change your resources and creation then succeed + succeed + succeed = we have a new creation to work with and develop.

Start again see what you get the second or ninth time around. Consider the first times brainstorming and breaking through YOUR limitations. Have a cookie, cookies make things yummy.

This is great for those that have expansive ideas.

Good execution is also excellent to have. Many limit or stop at the attraction stage because they do not carry through. Desire doesn't care if you stop in the attracting phase. Desire continues on leaving those that fail to carry through with their concepts, frustrated because they did not complete what they started. Similar to almost having an orgasm.

Do you function well enough in the third dimension to materialize your desire? Be honest with yourself. What issues do you need to address before you have what it takes to materialize a creation in the third dimension?

Many limit or stop at the attraction stage because they lack carry through skills, they didn't master them as a child. Their fear or limits or old patterns took over and nothing past talk gets manifested.

Are you nursing a wound or injustice that takes much of your manifesting energy? Is your manifesting energy being used to create drama or a "pity party" or are you repeating the same speech over and over?

Are you spending all your manifesting energy to get another person to love and approve of you? Tsk Tsk

As dear Suze Orman says, until women and some men learn to love and give to THEMSELVES FIRST as well as they give to others they will NEVER be powerful in their personal OR their business life. The world does not VALUE what you do until YOU value you and what you DO or create.

When you can't keep the "I AM" going twenty four seven…Stop what you are doing and master that first. If you fall in any of the above categories HANDLE that BEFORE you work on manifesting with your small bit of left over energy, it is not enough to bother with. And who says, "size doesn't matter."

MANIFESTATION stage:

MANIFESTING brings your ideas from the unseen or concept stage into matter into the third dimension. We do this UNCONSCIOUSLY all the time in our lives. That is how you conned Mom into making cookies for you. When you thought about how wonderful it would be to have a cookie to eat, Ah, but what kind, you asked and pleaded and offered to do something for her and before you knew it you were eating cookies. How bad can that be. For your business it is good to consciously manifest what you want.

Desire continues on leaving those people that stopped before manifesting frustrated, with their energy all in a wade because they did not complete what they started. So we will probably hear them run their mouths for ever with little or no action to back them up.

If I could only figure out how to get a chocolate cake to eat. The things you fail to own start creating on their own. Frequently they start creating "issues" to get your attention. Your issues like to see how many times you can do the same thing and still pretend it has nothing to do with you.

Another way to view the above is that YOU are sabotaging YOURSELF because you have not cleared up your life issues by OWNING THEM before you started to create. Creating a business is for people with their ducks in a row BEFORE they create. Otherwise you bring your "ISSUES" into the creation. That is what the energy of OLD ENERGY is all about. Your issues!

You give some thought to your issues now while the rest of us move on to manifesting.

***

As we proceed to manifest using pure raw energy that transforms itself into mathematical equations and then into a type of logic. AH! but the logic itself doesn't hold the answers.

The SOURCE energy is coming from *us, the creators.*

We created the universe, those of us that are the imaginers and dreamers, the angelic beings who came to Earth by lowering their energy. They created the potentials and ultimately the reality in third dimension, matter. The earth became what we all agreed as a group it would become.

CLEAR is the color of the new energy and it is not negative or positive. New energy is NON vibrational. AH! but it is expansional and O P E N moving in and out of the dimensions and is available energy to help create dynamic changes in the world of business.

Some directions to consider.

Revolutions of consciousness are being brought into business by the world wide web. There is almost an infinite amount of energy and money available to play with if you believe in, accept and allow the resources to come to you. Very new ideas and thoughts are available to be created with, when we refrain from suppressing and doubting them.

VIEW IN A NEW WAY:

There are new concepts in banking about getting "seed money" and where it comes from and how it is acquired. You can even be your own bank if you like.

Lawyers what is there to say about them, can you make one of them a friend to your business? I think they are lonely people.

You come up with your own creative way to incorporate these aspects in your business. Maybe a large coffee and cookie party could be a start.

Awareness and spiritual consciousness is here to stay, so do not loose sight of that. The angelic realm is considering themselves partners with us to move energy in the third dimension. Angelic realm considers themselves our supporters and backup. Well aren't they doing LOTS of shepherding and herding and what a messenger service they are, and who does better synchronicity than the angelic realm. MY MY MY they are excellent. They are the omniverse messengers, does it get any bigger and better than that—I don't know but I guess its possible.

Sales and MARKETING *is* communication.

COMMUNICATION is not arm twisting, brow beating, tricking or seducing your consumer, that is old energy. Ethics my dear, integrity and ethics is what your business needs. It is essential to be credible and truthful. If you need to con or trick people to use or buy your product it is time to move in a different direction or start with a new creation.

When you need to force or trick someone to buy what you have to sell it will backfire on you.

Communicate that you have something to offer.

Be on time to meetings. Keep your promises or just do not make promises when you cannot keep them. Respond promptly when you are addressed. Look clearly at the core energy of things you are dealing with and incorporate that awareness into your project.

PAPERWORK, competitors, **Governments:**

The government you live within is the collective consciousness of all the people in that area. Gracefully pay your fees and taxes as they support the government you reside in and that in turn supports your business. One hand washes the other. Before sending documents and paperwork into agencies or government offices, bless them and you bless your creation.

Barriers or challenges or other countries are good to meld with. That way you can add their energy to your enterprise and they benefit from your energy contribution or sharing.

Keep yourself aware of any areas of friction. Incorporate those areas of friction into your discussions so you can create new methods or ideas for resolution. Help shape the rules and laws governing your business by breaking things down into small manageable chunks. You might need to redefine or get very literal at times in your business to keep everyone on the same page.

Restructuring an OLD ENERGY business could be a large frustration.

First, you will need to know if there is a willingness to evolve out of old ways. Are they capable of viewing things in a new way? Is having more consciousness, self respect and integrity a goal the old energy business can live with. Are the bosses and managers able to value workers and vendors on the same level they value and honor themselves.

Contracts are only starting potentials, beginning contracts work that way. They get the ball rolling to help in the decision process. To change or not change contracts and agreements— meetings go on all the time in the unseen world about what would be best. Every step of the way there are conversations about the direction to go and the people to include or exclude. There is a good deal of patience as long as there is at least some moving and evolving. When the unseen world sees you too frozen to keeping evolving. They just STOP their involvement and turn their attention to something else that is moving.

They will check in on you but they are done while you wallow in a low vibration of some sort of fear or worry you created.

Past life residue, a *contract* or a MISSION

A small point of clarification: The difference between a past life residue, a contract or a mission.

ALL CONTRACTS are based on windows of opportunity which are action items for you individually. Planned in *compassion for your enlightenment.*

When you do not know the difference between a cellular intuitive feeling, or past life residue and a mission start to walk into it to find out what it is to you. Your discernment will tell you.

When you remove yourself from situations that are not spiritual you make a profound statement to the universe and it smiles at you. When you sit in a heap worried and fearful about what you were supposed to do NOTHING will happen. Only when you step out of your fear and INTO action will your lesson be engaged and your business thriving.

***

Forget all you used to know about business because odds are it will be rather different in the new energy, just as you are different in the new energy. Keep your sense of humor alive.

Use you humor as a *creative tool.*

Laughter is an energy EXCHANGER.

Joy and laughter should be happening frequently at work as it helps the invisible realm help you. Laughter gets the quantum physics of your business flowing out into the cosmos, increasing supportive options.

Hang your shingle out and get a business card as they are symbolic things that might help YOU feel you have a business and ANNOUNCES to all above and below that you are in fact in business.

You are an energy to be reckoned with.

When finances are not available to you in the moment take a walk and breathe. Have clarity about your business until the money or support comes to you. You realize that when starting up a business there is frequently long hours and many challenges, yes?

You have a team of angelic beings at your disposal to network with along with all the humans. When you set something in motion allow it the freedom to flow in its own direction. Work with your heart and soul. Energy moves, expands and re-balances ITSELF, work *with* that and use it to your advantage.

On your computer or on the physical desk top you might want to keep a group of suggestions or ideas at the ready. Allow everyone to access the suggestions and be able to contribute and / or consult. Putting the ideas out and grouped allows the ideas to affect each other and get reconfigured if that would please them. See what the fermentation process or flow can produce now and again.

A heads up. When you fail to check on the ideas they might get lost to others or just go away.

TEAM BUILDING and feeling everyone's energy contribution is valued and needed is important. Bonding is most important to the humans, you know how isolated we all feel. Remember to come from your heart awareness when dealing with all the entities that touch your business.

When you do not know what to do next in your business consider walking away from it for a little bit. Take a vacation or do something else the business might well be in an **incuba-**

tion process at this time the synchronicity needs time to line up. Consult the invisible realms time line. Their time line is frequently different than the humans time line.

This is the end of the third great era on earth the Christos era and the starting of the new era of consciousness or realization is here. In this era business and spirituality will become our new governments.

We can adopt a belief system and then manifest it.

Consider the belief system to be a factory. Feed the factory with beliefs of your choice and that is what you will create more of. Belief systems will become everything. There will be no need to control events and people to get what you are after. Just decide what you want and experience that.

Just DO SOMETHING!

Open your links and let your energy flow. See a grander picture. Tremendous change is happening. Stay in your space and expand yourself very far out if you wish to take in all you want.

When you are out networking and interacting with other people, you change their potentials for the rest of the day. They alter your potentials also. So many different potentials and so many people affecting each other, their lives get changed, what a fascinating chaos.

Having faith in yourself gives you faith in all humankind.

What happens to you or what you think is all a matter of perspective.

Your self love is equal to the value you put on all human potential.

Without the higher perspective you cannot conceive of the higher potential and consequently the higher perspective cannot be manifested.

Your skill at imagining, creating and manifesting will become the core energy of your business. The new government and religion of the world will become the business of IMAGINING, **creating** and *manifesting*.

***

Some profit-generating activities of a business.

For example:

Manufacturers produce products from raw materials or component parts which are then sold at a profit. Companies making physical goods, such as vehicles or plastics are considered manufacturers.

SERVICE BUSINESSES offer intangible goods or services and typically generate a profit by charging for labor or other services provided. Organizations ranging from tour guides to consulting firms or restaurants and even to entertainers are types of service businesses.

Retailers and Distributors act as middlemen in getting goods produced by manufacturers to the intended consumer generating a profit as a result of providing sales or distribution services. Most consumer-oriented stores and catalogue companies are distributors or retailers.

Agriculture and mining businesses are concerned with the production of raw material such as plants or minerals.

FINANCIAL BUSINESSES include banks and other companies that generate profit through investment and management of capital.

Information businesses generate profits primarily from the resale of intellectual property and include movie studios, publishers and packaged software companies.

Utilities produce public services such as heat, electricity, or sewage treatment, and are usually government chartered.

REAL ESTATE businesses generate profit from selling, renting and development of properties, homes, and buildings.

Transportation businesses deliver goods and individuals from location to location generating a profit on the transportation costs.

There are many other divisions and subdivisions of businesses.

The authoritative list of business types for North America is generally considered the North American Industry Classification System, or NAICS. The equivalent European Union list is the NACE.

***

For centuries, alchemists have sought to change base metals into gold. But the transmutation of metals like lead into gold is symbolic of a higher and more noble Alchemy—the Alchemy of self-transformation. SELF-TRANSFORMATION was the goal of most spiritual of alchemists.

CREATE in the NOW moment with your *thoughts* of what will be in the future. Whenever you find yourself in any difficult situation you can move forward in time to see and create an outcome. To walk backward in time in a linear time frame and you jump into the future.

The invisible realm says, they cannot change our life. They cannot change our world. All they can do is help us remember who we are. We are looking for a reflection and validation of the truth we all carry within us.

✳✳✳

CHAPTER 4

BRAIN OVERLOAD

Brain overload is dangerous to your sanity.

Your personal nuttiness can easily be the result of you denying parts of you that you have not approved of historically. Then, there are the parts of you that have been used against your by others, frequently by a parent or two, to torment you. This usually starts in childhood. So you decide without these parts you would be a much happier and loved-person. If life worked better by getting rid of parts of you that you do not like, that would be a most excellent plan.

I want to assure you that if you are seeking an internal peace, things absolutely DO NOT work like that.

We absolutely need to embrace the parts of us that we hate. We must embrace the parts we feel betrayed us. It really is the only way to go, I promise.

A little more history to consider.

As you look around at people you may see there is *more depression* and nutty behavior than you have ever seen before. This might well be due to the added stress of having our brains rewired at this time.

Now the rewiring starts for all humans.

Many light workers have been going through the rewiring for the past five years.

Compassion for everyone is needed more than ever before. There is always chaos when humans are confronted with change. We do not do change well at all. Yet we get bored without change.

Everything is the journey there IS NO DESTINATION, **we are eternal.**

We keep thinking we are humans looking for a spiritual awakening, when actually we are a SPIRITUAL BEINGS trying to cope with a HUMAN AWAKENING. We are trying to figure out what we came here to do.

Looking for answers is a good thing.

As we search for answers, the two lobes of the brain start communicating in different and new ways. This transference of energy between the two lobes helps our soul to search for answers within the physical body. When we ponder a question having no simple answer, the brain builds new synaptic pathways that actively search for the answer we seek.

When we talk to the unseen world enabling spiritual communication, our brain seeks that connection through newly formed synaptic pathways. When we begin to channel we increase the number of synaptic pathways. People who seem to have a good ability to talk to spirit actually have an ability to quickly build new synaptic pathways. It is not actually the number of pathways that you have, but the activation of new ones that opens the communication we seek.

Our 90%er is rewiring and reworking the human brain and DNA , reconnecting all twelve loops. This is an evolutionary cycle, nothing awful is happening. The brain needed to be separated to give the brain the illusion of duality. The illusion and the veil exists between the two halves of our brain. We have made the veil so thick we forgot we are spirits having a human experience.

The LEFT SIDE of the brain marks **linear time** and gives us the *game we are playing.* The left side **pretends to be human** and quantifies everything and puts it in boxes. The human thinks it is human when it is only spirit playing a game. See how creative spirit has been.

RIGHT SIDE of the brain is the **creative side**, with the concept of NOW time. The *right side of the brain is infinite* because it is God. It is the soul moving into the human that is causing our biology to change to accommodate it. Spiritual enlightenment is not following any human. Soul all ready knows that, You Are God Also.

With the new fiber optic cables we are getting more **light and information** carried to us. In the days ahead, what is call channeling and spirit communication will become commonplace. *We all have that ability all of the time.* With the new fiber optic cables this will not be a problem and everyone will discover their inner connection to spirit. We have only scratched the surface in our sciences to understand what light is all about.

Our physical changes are happening to help us move from duality to being interdimensional. We are starting to sense and feel the shadows of other dimensions and realities.

We are playing this game to define or see God because in an infinite state God cannot study itself. By wearing a body, God can see who she is, and see how she behaves and defines herself. We are not the only God. There are many Gods on this planet.

Only the highest vibrating angels came to earth at this time.

As you vibrate higher everyone around you matches your vibration. This is a good thing fear it not as fear is only the energy of the unknown. Once you know the unknown fear leaves.

Reincarnation weaves the web of life with BILLIONS of life forms interacting throughout time and space including "now time." All these life forms make the universe and our life stream more complicated and complex. That means each being is not only itself it is also composed of the remnants of those which came before it. Yes, how easy is it to clarify all that.

Within each being is another being and another being within that being, creating a vast chain of lives and awareness making up the intricate pattern of our spiritual past. All the remnants and bits of you that came before are imparting "their knowingness" we have, which should be unknown to us. Our impulses or lack of impulses, our knowledge or lack of knowledge we didn't realize we have come from ALL the remnants and bits of us. All the remnants of us and our energy excesses and depletion's are always trying to rebalance themselves and trying to create a unified whole.

We exist in twelve different dimensions and are having a minimum of twelve slightly different experiences as one soul. Twelve different expressions of one soul on this planet simultaneously. What if you left one life in one dimension and went to another dimension to consult with another part of your soul for answers or awareness to an issue you had. Would you come back refreshed and renewed, with a new multidimensional consideration?

Your path was laid out for you by you.

We need to **expand our thoughts and feelings.**

There are times the physical body needs **grounding** *to keep you on earth* and in your body. There are many ways to refresh the body using water, food, sunlight, intimacy, sex, nurturing and touch. When the body is not grounded enough for the **rewiring process** the body gets OVERLOADED.

WHEN the **hypothalamus gland** overproduces, the ungrounded physical body produces illnesses like Chronic Fatigue Syndrome and Fibromyalgia. These energy disorders are likely to increase on the planet.

Your first experience with multidimensionality could cause you to lose grounding and YOU COULD GET STUCK between energetic **dimensions.** Your 90%er might create one of theses energetic illnesses because you cannot move forward until you have fully received the **gift** *of the illness.* Which may be that it is time to slow down and smell the roses, or pay attention to that lonely isolated child of yours, or stop neglecting your spouse.

Probably it is time to communicate with your 90%er.

The other behavior that will help a great deal at this time is to *gather all the parts of you that you have cast off* because you didn't approve of them. Maybe you have abused or have been abused, or you could have an addiction you have not owned. You might consider the judgmental part of you no good and deny it. Some reject their sexuality or their entire body. The child or a fearful person's reasoning might be "If I did not have a body" no one could do things to it that I do not want done.

You might of **given a part of you away** to someone you loved, needed or wanted. Then there are those that just TAKE what they want. They mistakenly believe they can hold onto you by using force which never works for long.

Please, the time has come to welcome all your parts and pieces back and meld yourself all together as one.

When we own and embrace all our parts and bits it is so much *easier to maintain our balance.* Remember to avoid judging your parts regardless what those parts have been doing. Your parts or at least their energy come and present themselves to you so you can own them and listen to what they have to say. There will be parts from this life and past lifetimes and even before that showing up. They want **acknowledgment** and to *share the wisdom* they gained on *your behalf.* Then they would like you, "their creator" to bless and release them so they can continue on their own way.

IT never, NEVER goes the other direction you cannot deny a part of you exists first and then that part of you will go away. When you deny a part of yourself it will start causing you trouble. The disowned part starts lying to you because that is what YOU request it to do.

Just as when you show displeasure at a child's behavior the child starts to lie to you because it wants to please its parent. Your disowned part lies to you because it wants to please its creator.

Many humans at this time are coping with a degree of mental unbalance because of the large degree of energy being sent to earth. There is a large increase of awareness being sent to the entire planet.

The increase of energy is *overwhelming the* BRAIN.

The physical sensations of large amounts of energy coming into the HEAD are felt as **PRESSURE** in the head or one might have the SENSATION of *whirling* or *dizziness.*

The way to rebalance yourself and all that energy coming in IS A LOT of **deep breathing.** You can also consider allowing that energy to enter your ENTIRE BODY instead of limiting the energy to only entering the head. It is perfectly fine and rather desirable to allow the new energy to flow in through ALL PARTS of your body that is how the energy *wants* to come into you. It does not want to be RESTRICTED to only the brain.

BREATHE my dear, breath deeply.

OLD ENERGY: Things went rather slow and outcomes were easily anticipated. We split ourselves up into acceptable and unacceptable parts. Expanded the brains job description too large for it to handle.

NEW ENERGY: Things are going on so rapidly and in so many different directions we must meld all our rejected aspects into one. Allow energy to entire all areas of the body and embrace all our rejected parts.

BREATHE your pieces back into you.

Historically, there has been a slow steady flow of energy or awareness coming through our bodies resulting in a rather *small amounts* of nutty behavior or thought in the general population.

The times mental unbalance increases in the population is when there is a *greater amount of awareness* coming in like it is now and when there is almost **no awareness** coming in as in the dark ages. Those on the edge of unbalance get pushed over into being very unbalanced when there is an increase or decrease of energy.

There is so much SPIRITUAL CONSCIOUSNESS flowing in at this time it is overloading the mind, especially the mind of all ready fragile souls. Actually the energy is trying get the human to open *their hearts* and other parts of their body and to stop relying so heavily on the brain. The brain is NOT designed to understand the invisible realm or spirituality yet.

The brain cares for the body.

At this time if the pressure in the brain gets too great it WILL CAUSE mental unbalance and the unseen world seems okay with that. Their priority is for humans to open their heart and if mental unbalance is created in the process SO BE IT. The greater concern is the heart or spiritual awakening.

Soul wants you to open your heart, it can be done easy or hard your choice. Soul is 90% of who you are. How wise is it to fight your ninety percent?

This is a time of VERY increased spiritual consciousness.

Lost balance between the angelic levels and human levels tend to make the human not know how to work with their own energy anymore. **When humans shut off these corresponding energies, they go crazy.** They get unbalanced and tend to have a twisted, dark, depressed, sexual energy within them. They tend to go feeding because **they have been fed on** also. They will go after those who they consider to be holders of more pure energy.

***

MEDICATION for brain overload.

Medication can work on some of the symptoms of mental unbalance but does NOT work on the causes of the unbalance. No matter how hard you reject a part of you that you do not approve of on your own or with medication you will still need EVENTUALLY to own and meld with THAT PART of you at some point. Medication will only delay the melding.

***

UNBALANCED or retarded as your CHOICE

There are times when people CHOOSE to come into a body mentally unbalanced or even retarded as a self punishment for things they have done in past lifetimes. So, being mentally unbalanced or retarded is the method they picked to rebalance their energy.

Some PICK mental unbalance as a way to AVOID **allowing** the brain too much power so they can develop their heart center or spiritual consciousness especially if they HAD abused others mentally in past lives.

Helen Keller chose to come in blind, deaf and mute so she could learn to expand into new dimensions. And her parents and teacher agreed to assist her. It was all contracted ahead of time.

Some decide to take on mental unbalance on behalf of another person or all of humanity in a service role.

***

MIND CONTROL

"Mind control" is a term used to label methods of extreme coercion that result in an individual's INVOLUNTARY, RO-BOTIC COMPLIANCE. During Atlantis up through present time there has been mind control. There are rituals explicitly describing methods of torture and intimidation to create trauma based mind control. Drugs are used frequently and casting spells (hypnosis) ultimately resulting in total enslavement of the initiate.

When a person is in a drugged or a dissociated state they are highly suggestible. Females can be turned into slaves of one sort or another. Males into killers or handlers of other mind control victims. This training is handed down in cult families generation after generation since at least the 1300s and is done world wide. The "training" is sometimes done before birth and to most cult family infants.

When undergoing trauma induced by electroshock there is a feeling of lightheadedness evidenced. As in "Project Monarch" they used trauma structured dissociation and occult integration in order to compartmentalize the mind into multiple personalities within a systematic framework that "the handler" could access and use for a large variety of activities. None benefiting the mind control slave.

Sometimes a satanic ritual is performed with the express purpose of attaching a particular demon or group of demons to the corresponding alter(s). The fear created was for easier control and convincing the individual that they were evil (1-5 year olds) and had no control over their own body. They were told satan owned them and controlled their body.

There are an inordinate amount of alters in a victim or survivor with numerous back-up programs, mirrors and shadows. A division of lightside (good) and darkside (bad) alters are interwoven in the mind and rotate on an axis. There are seven levels each having an internal programmer who oversees things, or the "gatekeepers" who grants or denies entry into the different rooms. This is all located in the brain of a victim, it is their own virtual personal reality.

There can also be non-biological twinning which is when they put two very young non-related children in a ceremony or ritual to be "soul-bonded" inseparably paired for eternity. They essentially share two halves of the same programmed information making them interdependent.

Research has found that in, dissociative identity disordered individuals, you find more pronounced para normal phenomenon, astral projection, telepathy and ESP than found in the normal population.

Beta waves are usually given off during normal waking activity.

With theta waves or twilight, there is a lot of endorphins released making a person feel good. This is usually the same state we all have just before sleep or when you get hypnotized driving. Theta activity is also associated with the ability to rapidly ABSORB and LEARN INFORMATION.

With theta waves there is **UNCRITICAL ACCEPTANCE** of *verbal material*. For programmers to get a trainee to the theta frequency they use rapid flashing lights, drugs, phased sound waves, negative ions (electromagnetic energy fields) electroshock, alterations in gravity in the cerebellum (spinning), microwave emitters, and lasers.

Programming success depends on **altering the child's** or the adult's perception of it's *five senses*. Current electronic technology makes TORTURING people physically obsolete to program them. Trauma based programming is no longer necessary to access altered brain states.

Sadly there are a large number of humans that just enjoy torturing others when they can and many are parents.

Unless suicide programs are disconnected they are easily activated when therapy is tried. There are sleep programs designed to shut down the individual if their mind starts to remember any of their programing.

Programming information from **Brice Taylor:**

If my subconscious mind threatened to divulge secrets, my father had programmed me to "wake and eat chocolate chip cookies to remember to forget". Should I begin to remember the secret activities I would stub my big toe or burn myself on the stove thereby redirecting my focus. I also had personalities that reported on what I did, if it was out of line. I reported on myself.

Her mom was programmed to sleep through or she was drugged or in a dissociative daze when her child was being abused or being beaten by her husband or any others. Mom never was consciously aware of what was happening to herself or her daughter.

As Brice Taylor was deprogrammed she often mentally bumped into spin, sleep, suicide, migraine and drug programs she had to **fight through** in order to get to the MEMORY of the original experience. I (Brice Taylor) was often physically sick as the program dictates and suffered massive migraine headaches and pain in different parts of my body while retrieving information.

My programing required that I was *food, liquid deprived* before and during the time of my use. Often they paired electric shock with bright lights and music or word phrases. At our grade school and high school there was an **inner group of teachers** and faculty whose goal was to "enhance our minds".

No one realized I wasn't operating in a conscious state, that I had been programed, drugged and electric shocked to maintain THETA BRAIN WAVE patterns so I could retain VAST AMOUNTS OF DATA.

The same routine was used to be sure I was amnesiac of every thing. Trauma, isolation, food and sleep deprived. I was a TOTAL robot programed NOT to respond to pain and torture which many of the men subjected me to over and over again. I never could figure out why I was so exhausted and in pain the next day.

By 1980 time had shown the controllers that **TRAUMA itself** was one cause of programming breakdown in slaves. They started doing more training via computer screen and virtual reality. Children are force feed information into previously set up inner systems of mind files and are trained to accept vast amounts of highly technological information starting at 3 years.

Brice Taylor has also said: Now they can do surgery with energy and no incision. They can insure a body doesn't disease by monitoring the electromagnetic field variations. The public isn't being informed.

***

Inmates were heavily targeted for reprogramming in the early 70s.

Preschoolers were heavily targeted for reprogramming in the late 70s.

During the time of Atlantis we discovered how easy it was to control others mentally with mind control. Some of us ran amuck with their control and manipulation the same way some of our government programers have done AGAIN during this lifetime.

The government programming in Atlantis resulted in a total disconnect of the persons SOUL and the **human self**. When there is a total disconnect the human self finds it *impossible to stay compassionate or balanced* when not connected to the soul. They revert to beast like behavior in extreme cases.

Some of the slaves (beasts) in Atlantis have carried their programming forward into this lifetime. They have not been able to shake that overlay in all the lifetimes since Atlantis, they have remained mentally unbalanced. They have remained earthbound and tormented between lifetimes also. Between lives the suffering was even greater for these people so they kept coming back in human form.

The individuals that put these mind control metal bands (called crowns) on other humans are suffering the same fate during this lifetime as the slaves have suffered all this time.

Those that hurt themselves and or others are haunted by their own loss of spiritual connection.

To heal these individuals, to get the human self to release the illusion of having **no soul**, is no small task. One way to heal them would be for them to go back to a time when they were connected with spirit and reexperience what that felt like. This would mean for some going back to the early days of Atlantis before the metal band was placed on their head. Then the reconnection might take years to ground and be accepted and rebalanced.

You say you want to help?

This is a time to call in **experts.** Unless you know what you are doing it would probably make them furious and more irrational when they learned what was done to them. Accepting with grace is not the beasts strong suit. Could you handle the intense venting and possible physical violence? I think probably not.

Safest approach to helping these mentally unbalanced might be to get them breathing deeply. They will fight you. The breathing stimulates their energy to reconnect with their life force and declares a will to live with awareness. When they value their life they might also come to value yours, MAYBE.

A word to those who try to control their own minds with "positive good thoughts" only. How does one decide if a thought is positive or negative without a judgment of that thought? And how large is your frame of reference? The ability to fail or think negatively as well as the ability to succeed and think positively is rather subjective and subject to change.

Combining the opposites together is true expansion.

Affirmations and visualization do not work because they come from the limitations of the mind. True consciousness goes far beyond what the mind can ever imagine.

Bullies are created by bully parents that teach separation, bigotry, and misuse of personal power. Where do you learn it is acceptable to hurt others? At home of course.

✣✣✣

DISSOCIATIVE Identity Disorder

Certain disorders blend the physical and psychological difficulties a person might have. Remembering and forgetting are taken for granted until there is a problem in that area do we recognize the power of memory. The moments we remember and events we forget create the fabric of mystery and tragedy that can shatter our confidence and make us question what we THINK we know.

In the dissociated person the CORE PERSONALITY is hiding *deep inside* the person. If you want to help you could try to coax the core personality to come back out of its hiding place and reconnect with all its parts in an effort to rebalance itself. In my experience making all the parts aware of each others existence, all having co-consciousness makes the core personality a bit braver and sometimes brave enough to come out and resume ownership.

The unseen world can be a great help in creating co-consciousness in all the parts by telling you how many parts there are and what jobs they have been assigned or roles they have to play. For instance when the individual is fearful one part will take over and deal with that. If there is abuse a different part may come forward to deal with that. When the person is in overwhelm a part is broken off and isolated to deal with that specific issue.

I had a student with multiple personalities and only one of them knew how to read, the other two didn't even like school.

Those affected with dissociation might not realize some of their personalities might well have been brought from a past life or two or three to deal with a current life issue. They often assume someone is out to persecute them during this lifetime when it is only an old aspect of THEM that is taking over.

The human is only 10% of our multiple self and the top one on the pile of our pastlives is the one having control of all the other lives. Often we DO feel past life residue in our DNA. Our DNA does not always know it has moved to another body and has different concerns in this lifetime.

ALL HUMANS are really only a small part of a "group entity" in two different directions. The multiple past lifetimes lived and the fact that a human in ANY lifetime is only 10% of all our other invisible parts.

The human along with their invisible 90% conglomerate are also part of the cosmic intelligence of all things. With the new energy that is almost finished arriving on earth, all of us at our individual rates will slowly start remembering all our other parts unless we deny them, when they come calling. Through the ascension process they all do come calling at one time or another. It will not be an overnight thing. We will be remembering our parts bit by bit.

***

AUTISM

The autistic lack the SPONTANEOUS SHARING most of us engage in. They are **impaired** in their ability to initiate or sustain conversation with others. They lack emotional affect because they do not have the emotions we do, so why would they respond like the rest of us. Their lack of emotion is hard to be comfortable with because you do not know what they are feeling or thinking.

The autistics **emotional bonds** are to PLACES or *objects* with specific memories rather than to a person. They use their intellect and **logical** decision making for every *social decision*. Emotions do not guide their behavior, pure computation does.

Physical touch can CONFUSE, **hurt** or upset the autistic person. They are not so good at multitasking either and as Dr. Temple Grandin says the autistic thinking is similar to many animals thinking in the close attention they pay to detail. For instance an object being out of place bothers them and can make them fearful, like a bag or cup something the rest of us might not even notice. www.grandin.com.

Autistic THINKING is **rigid** they have limited ability to generalize. Autistic accomplish tasks by going through a series of memorized pictures they can't alter or restructure so they can't come up with alternative behaviors or solutions unless they rehearse them in advance.

When asked to relay a story the autistic *associational visual thinker* rambles off a plotless story that doesn't have a clear beginning, middle or end.

Rapid shifting of their attention between two different stimuli is VERY DIFFICULT for them and in some autistics impossible. They use ONE *sensory channel* at a time. That is why they have trouble making eye contact AND talking at the same time. They can do one or the other not both together, comfortably. They may have repetitive motor function like flapping or twisting and preoccupation with a part of an object.

Large groups of autistics develop normally until two to seven years at that time they will start to lose their speech. They might become withdrawn or quiet to PREVENT **sensory overload**. Either a sibling or parent of an autistic child will have delayed speech and / or learning problems 42% of the time. Other common traits found in families of autistics are anxiety disorder, depression, bipolar, and panic attacks.

Autistic have a hard time judging the **INTENTIONS** of others. Their nervous system is constantly *stressed* so they become hyper vigilant. This anxiety fuels fixations and acts as a motivator OR prevents action.

Some autistics have a near normal brain trapped inside a sensory system that doesn't work with the ease our sensory system dose. There are three types of sensory processing problems;

extremely oversensitive, very UNDER SENSITIVE and internal white noise interference.

They have *intense knowingness* and do not know how to handle what they see in the world outside of them. They may well see more going on than we do. To cope with the confusion they feel they will go internal. When they stare off into space they may well be seeing and participating in *interdimensional attributes* of life until we interfere with all our "shoulds." They can "see" other life on earth the life we do not acknowledge yet.

Asperger's syndrome is a milder form of autism. The adult is generally ill groomed and BLUNT, talks with *tension* and a nervous rasp. They talk with complete self absorption and little thought for the *comfort or interest of the listener.*

They are not able to feel what you feel. They want to produce **something concrete** and are not interested in drama or how someone else feels. They are too self enclosed to be tolerant of others wishes or concerns.

They need the love and encouragement of their parents and friends if they have them and teachers would be wise to help them understand their **gift of sensitivity.**

They remember or have a knowingness of language being made up of sounds and vibrations. The languages used during the time of Atlantis were singing languages. Now we form symbols through our mouth which sound very flat.

Go outside the box with autistic. Encourage singing and rejoicing for them. They need to feel they are in a safe space.

They wish to communicate and live outside of linearity.

They would love to communicate without verbal speech.

Language to them is in a bubble like an E-mail is to us. They would rather do language all it once in a shoud, using group think to communicate.

The souls choosing to come into a body with Autism are interested in being ENERGY PIONEERS. They are **independent and blessed** with a new consciousness that functions beyond the mind and emotions.

Maybe they are a bit less human than we are. They are not swayed much by what other humans want for them or project on them.

The autistic bunch are rather independent and hypersensitive to many things we have no problem with.

In the new energy the autistic are mostly savants. The children are born with *magnetically enhanced DNA* compared to ours. They are more geared to an interdimensional existence.

Our way of life is frustrating to them because their expansiveness is always being limited by us trying to force them into their heads instead of just being free to feel or sense.

There is communication at a distance between autistic children and sea mammals like dolphin and whales. If they establish a one-on-one relation to a single animal that will last a lifetime.

An autistic person is multidimensional and lives with one foot in two worlds. In fact, they may exist more in the other world than in third dimension. The biggest challenge a person with autism experiences is the frustration and possibly anger they might feel. They have so much information coming in that they cannot fully interpret it. Those of us who are not autistic have filters in place that allow you to only see and experience the information and vibrations within your own reality. Autistic people have those filters removed, and they have a difficult time assimilating information the same way we do. This is beginning to change as a result of our own dimensional shift and opening to multidimensionality with the rewiring process now underway.

The autistic child can speak to, or talk through a crystal because it is a translation device, because it exists in multiple dimensions itself. Not all crystals can be used to reach autistic children, but ones of the correct vibration have been used for this purpose. This is similar to the fact that most autistic children can communicate with some animals and particularly with those we know to be multidimensional, such as dolphins. Understand that there are translation devices that already exist and have for some time. This will now start to happen with other forms as well. Some will be objects and some will be living, multidimensional forms of life.

See autistic for the possibilities that they hold.

***

HYPNOSIS

Can be used as a method of memory retrieval but is unreliable. In a hypnotic trance a person is in a state of relaxed wakefulness which can make a person more compliant but not always. Hypnosis can alter mood, blood flow, perception and memory.

Hypnosis is **programing on top of programing** and consequently NOT A CURE for much of anything. Hypnosis is always an overlay and never a solution.

Experiments conducted by experts have proven that a person awake is better able to retrieve their memories than a hypnotized person can.

Hypnosis *reduces ones free will.*

***

SELF-CUTTER

Self-cutting is repetitive, nonleathal cutting of the body. Cutting indicates problems, trauma in this lifetime or past lifetimes. More females than males cut on themselves. Males get into more vehicle accidents than females do. With cutting it is common to find personality disorders or an eating disorder along with the cutting behavior.

Self abuse is frequently used to see how alive you are FEELING. Some mentally unbalanced have lost their feelings and their passions as a result of separation and lost contact with their soul. The cutter feels removed from their body and the cutting helps them get back into the body. Maybe they consider cutting as a way to call up the soul.

Cutting transforms invisible **EMOTIONAL** pain into a **physical** pain that can be seen and treated and accepted easier by many humans.

Cutters feel calmer and more relaxed after cutting. In childhood they felt calmer after being abused because the abuse happened and they no longer needed to be hyper vigilant looking for signs of when and how it would happen. It happened, it was over and now they can rest for a short bit.

When they cut THEY have the control. In the abusive situation they had no control.

There is self-hatred and anger for their lack of control over events in their lives. They judge and have disgust for their needs and feelings, they assume that is what got them into trouble in the first place. They want to be INDEPENDENT and **in control** of themselves not at the mercy of others in their life and do not feel strong enough to do that. Lots of conflict.

Self-cutting is frequently a coping mechanism brought from a pastlife, from abuses then.

***

DEPRESSION

Depression CAN BE used as a fuel to ascension.

Human depression that is not related to the ascension process is all about this lifetime. Depression is about the human getting into a very low energy wave or a slow vibration. This can happen with a physical challenge or pain, but is usually the person **absorbed** in HATING themselves.

Depression is an addiction to hanging onto and wallowing in the pain of "their old story."

The depressed person will get energized by talking about themselves and their suffering in THEIR STORY. A story about what they should be...What they ought to accomplish... and their SUPPRESSED anger at the self creates the depression they get stuck in.

One of the many reasons not to judge yourself, where is the benefit?

Releasing your *expectations* can release the depression. A sadness about something in your life can move into a depression. Depression can last three months to all lifetime or something in between.

***

A LARGE INFUSION OF SPIRITUAL ENERGY

Understanding how the HIGH INFUSION of spiritual energy affects us DOES help **calm the mind** down and then allows the BODY to rebalance itself without the mind getting panicky and interfering or trying to control things. A calm mind allows your 90%er to integrate smoothly with your human self with minimum upset and interference from the mind.

The mind can shut the body down or just goes CRAZY on some people.

The *mind is an energy center* and not a biological center necessarily. The mind moves energy, fluids and information throughout the body. Invite the mind to release its hold on everything and let it just chill out. The mind needs to learn how to share and allow the heart and soul to open up and take there place. When consciousness moves rapidly and the brain tries to limit the consciousness something BREAKS or gives way.

Currently our psychiatric methods and goals are no longer serving our needs. One could wonder if they ever have served anyone's needs. The psychiatric community seldom looks at childhood abuse and the patterns developed at home to heal adult issues and almost never allows looking at all beyond this lifetime or body for answers and information.

Now the human is being asked to merge gracefully with all their past lives and their soul along with all their spiritual awareness. A very tall order in a very short period of time with a human that is not so comfortable with change or new ideas or accepting there was existence before the current human life.

Those not mentally balanced are frequently working on other dimensions. The things they are going through and experiencing can be very real.

Mental unbalance can be created from:

The INSIDE of you, by YOU

From an energy outside of yourself.

Either way it results in an unbalance.

All the different energies are there for a reason.

With the speed which things are happening our spiritual discernment is even more critical needed than it has been in the past. Listen to your intuition or divine self to guide your actions. Those seeking a more heart centered path of expression while clinging to negative views and values will have a hard time establishing a higher level of morality and ethics.

When you can raise your morality and ethics in your own life by living with a higher moral standard that will in turn encourage those around you to raise their integrity.

Once we fully integrate our seven core chakras into the eighth chakra creating one unified chakra field we will move beyond passing everything through our heart. Our large unified chakra field connects us to our cosmic self the 90%er. At that time we will be walking harmlessly because we will fully feel God's vibration within our expanded body.

Use your discernment to determine what resonates for you personally. In a soul directed life that is a must. Hone your internal radar to FEEL your way through. Do what feels right to you, there is such a big difference between being self guided and going along to get along, being blocked by your personal fear.

The SOUL wants to express itself and it is bigger and badder than the mind. The soul is also aware of a great deal more than the mind is. The mind only believes in this lifetime.

To aid an overloaded brain pursue creative endeavors.

CREATIVITY will loosen the brain's control and fears the mind has. Creative projects get your energies flowing throughout the entire body instead of having the affect of continuous looping and stress the mind loves to engage in.

AS WE BECOME AWARE

As we become more aware as we work on our spiritual development remember to share what you are learning with your invisible entourage. When you read or learn new things ask if the entire entourage is understanding and when they do not, PLEASE clarify for them. They are in the same learning curve we are. Also, we all like to be consulted. You are the team leader and so you are responsible to all its members and their education along with them being responsible for your education, *spiritual of course.* Communicate, communicate, communicate and check for understanding frequently.

Because we are ascending so rapidly the entourage does not have a chance to stay abreast of all the new developments in the new energy because they are so busy being in service to us. Things are moving rapidly and in UNANTICIPATED ways. Please keep ALL your teem members informed and ask if there is ANYTHING you can get clarified for them. Compare what you feel and think with what they feel and think, you are acting as a unit now.

Check time lines frequently.

OLD ENERGY: Invisible realm cared for and watched over us.

NEW ENERGY: Invisible realm needs us to be sure to share with them all we learn and feel as they are learning after we do. We are putting it together for them and need to check frequently that they know what we are doing.

PEACE ON EARTH one soul at a time

Make peace and friends, heal borders no more walls. There are so many more levels in play than you are aware of. As the fear factors of ignorance and prejudice and superstition are decreasing from our life, science and spirituality will start to meet and merge. When science and spirituality are brought together the invisible will become known and change what is known about the visible.

Allow Divine Timing to play its role for all that happens is ultimately for your highest good.

The world looks on as our democracy is being eroded.

The major future potentials indicate that impeachment is needed or shall we continue to just limp along preaching fear to justify war. Several more weather crises and our President will affect America's economy more negatively than it already has. When our government starts to concern itself with what is best for ALL PEOPLE the weather crisis's can be a global orchestration of rescue, relocation and repair on the entire planet.

Our resources and manpower are needed for saving people rather than waging war. Start refusing to fight anymore, do not allow war in our collective consciousness. A global shift happens one heart at a time. Be willing to help each other in times of need, no matter whom you are or where the need may be. God's will is *simply to give and receive only love.* That is the one and only commandment in God's rule book.

Old energy all around us tends to bring us down literally draining our energy. So to work against brain overload rejuvenate the biology. Give the biology time and space to catch up with your consciousness. When your consciousness races forward your body's not sure what happened or what to do. The body is not totally balanced and harmonious our entire DNA and other aspects of the body are changing rapidly. Take many deep breathes.

You have one foot in the Old Energy. You have the other foot in the New Energy.

Speak your thoughts and feelings aloud, knowledge reduces confusion.

The work of a new energy person is difficult on the physical body and the mind. Our physical body tends to pick up much of the excess, stressed out of balance energy so treat your body very well.

****

BRAIN OVERLOAD AT DEATH

The ability to communicate with the invisible realm in our current life is a skill usually maintained after a human body dies. After death some types of knowledge we have stays, and some disappear. Specifics like names, dates, and places disappear along with many skills. Basic emotions and habits stay along with spiritual knowledge after death.

However spiritual abilities can be **obstructed** by a barrier between the soul and some types of knowledge that can cut the soul in two so things NORMALLY remembered are forgotten. *YOUR trauma or the infliction of trauma* on others WILL break the UNITY of the soul. Your own pain or another person's pain can sever the soul's access to that knowledge.

This does not happen with minor bad karma, which weighs down the soul and blurs its vision, but does not split it.

Ability to concentrate during life allows concentration to be maintained at the time of death. At death HABITS are maintained more easily than rational thought. Concentration allows our observation of the process of death and gives us conscious control over the speed of those events.

The ability we have to use our free will at death depends on the acceptance of the dying process and the ability to concentrate and focus attention during life. When the dying process is not accepted the soul becomes clogged with fear and other negative emotions making the pathway obstructed. Inability to concentrate means a large number of events seem to happen all at once with soul being dragged along in a semiconscious state. When the soul gets dragged along there are pieces of the self floating around and the person needs to keep himself together literally at the time of death.

The soul is an identity, a very unique identity. Soul is the expression of what you would call God or Spirit. The soul is your I AM, the overview of all that is visible and invisible, a divine wholeness. Your soul cannot be defined or structured or controlled. Soul has not been able to, or wanted to come into a limited, overly structured and suppressive environment where the mind rules and reality is inflexible.

The Brotherhood of Light can help at death if they are called.

They can protect the soul and unite its pieces as it is pulled through the vortex out of the realm of embodied existence and into the plane of spirits. Then the Brotherhood of Light can guide the soul to a more peaceful location giving it some options depending on its karma. When the soul doesn't have a goal it can get trapped waiting for something to happen. For these individuals the pain and upset of death will gradually lessen leaving the person in a gray world that is neither good nor evil but vague and insubstantial. Here they wait for the vortex of rebirth and get drawn into another womb and reincarnate in a new body.

CROSSING OVER

Eighty percent of those that die get lost in the fourth dimension or the gray world, where they frequently start the cycle of taking a body and going back to the fourth dimension and ultimately staying earth bound in the gray world that is neither good nor evil but vague and insubstantial. Of those that keep cycling from a body to the fourth dimension only ten percent are able to evolve out of that and get to the "bridge of flowers" on there own without help.

That means only twenty to thirty percent of those that die make their way to cross over the bridge of flowers. When you go to the bridge of flowers to cross over to the other side you can get more help and clarity and evolve spiritually before you come back to take another body. Currently they are also helping souls assimilate the new energy.

Those that do not cross over the bridge of flowers where they would gain some wisdom and help evolving spiritually, have issues or need help to evolve enough to cross over the bridge. Those in the gray world are not generally at peace with life or infinity. They might feel they had a wrongful death, are full of resentment or they may want to watch over particular people still in body or like my family members they are waiting for the "truck of happiness" to deliver happiness to them. If they had crossed over they would of become more spiritually evolved and aware enough to realize they needed to make themselves happy internally.

Happiness is not a gift bestowed on you externally from an outside source.

During the 1990s a call went out to humans to help cross over the earth bound souls stuck in the gray world. In the new energy the lost gray group, in the gray world that is neither good nor evil but vague and insubstantial were making a fair amount of static or were causing problems just as a virus does in a computer. They were over due for getting some assistance in accomplishing the change over from old to new energy also.

I have helped educate some of the earth bound predators and victims and those soul's with violent rages, to understand some of the psychology of those kind of behaviors. Their awareness was raised enough for me to get them to cross the bridge of flowers. That way they could get more personal assistance and in depth help to clear up their thinking about the "virtues" of victimhood, suffering and being predators.

They needed to know that to change their victimhood and suffering status they had to own their behavior. Accept responsibility for the way they reacted to what life gave them. They were doing those things to themselves.

When they gained the wisdom they wanted to get from that experience they can then release being a victim and suffering. Some very wrongly think that victimhood and suffering makes them more spiritual but the OPPOSITE is true. In their victimhood and suffering they are actually *rejecting their divine selves* and the soul tends to go away.

Apparently many aborted fetuses that had souls in the old energy were earth bound also. They were confused, lost and not feeling too loved. I comforted them and told them they served well. Then I crossed them over to the bridge of flowers. The end of February 2007, I crossed a large group, maybe a million or more of the aborted fetuses.

In early March 2007, my friend Dan and I crossed over some mentally retarded earth bound souls that wanted to cross. We crossed some still in a human body that were institutionalized and ready to go. They were confused and disoriented and they just didn't understand much of what was happening to them or why.

Mid March 2007, Dan and I crossed earth bound souls to the bridge of flowers, of angry divorced women. Yes I was also surprised at this category of souls locked into angry blaming because they were sexually abused as children and then got more of the same from their spouse. They are VERY ANGRY about their victimhood in their lifetime. They did not own any memory of them ABUSING in past lives, the same way they were abused this lifetime.

We talked many of them, not all of them, into transmuting their anger and blame enough to cross them over so they could gain more wisdom and get infused with the new energy.

The Brotherhood of Light supports people who have spiritual goals and spiritual travel is a method for attaining such goals. If a person is interested in traveling spiritually they need to develop a control mechanism for travel.

First, one needs to be able to escape the close identification with their physical body. Yogic concentration works or the barrier can be melted away by SHEER WILL. A tunnel or spiral can be visualized and passed through like opening a door or going through the third eye. When you have access to travel then you need to determine where to go and how to get there.

Each person and place has an identifier that you see. What you see is the karma organized as patterns not as a physical form but as an energy. While focusing your awareness on the person or place you need to shift your perceptions to perceive the underlying karmic structure rather than the physical person or place.

Yes, certain drugs will create a beautiful and decorative set of karmic images and geometric patterns the brain sees, which is limited and mind blowing and NOT SPIRITUAL. ON DRUGS You might well open yourself up to the lower world realms of desire and frustration, not areas that are recommended. The third dimension is more than enough frustration.

Visualizing a square or triangle mandala-like form is a safer more secure way to travel which also allows you to better control what happens. The physical world may be made into a background and appear flat. As a dark blue sky or ocean depths a vivid sunset pulls the imagination from physical objects.

Your heart must guide the soul towards SPIRITUAL GOALS and objects OR beings OR worlds and light.

When the soul transitions out of the body at death many things can happen. The soul may be weighed down by negative karma or it may be full of light and joy or it may end up in the uncertainty of the astral realms where good and bad balance each other and there is NO CLEAR and strong will. Most will go on their way to new lives in a body.

Some of the uncertain ones will meet with the Brotherhood of Light that travel by means of **light and sound** and they will help and council those souls. Some souls choose to stay and learn and they are willing to teach them. In the spiritual area the Brotherhood of Light teaches about the many different worlds the soul may enter and how to travel in the soul body.

OLD ENERGY: Invisible realm cared for and watched over us. In the spiritual area they taught about the many worlds the soul may enter and how to travel in the soul body.

NEW ENERGY: Humans stay where they are and expand out to any person or place they might want to interact with. We keep our entourage informed about what we are doing and changes that happen.

People have access to many worlds when they can focus on a particular person or place. This can occur spontaneously but is often a learned skill. As different bodies are associated with various sounds or forms of light. Your focus upon musical sound, different colors and intensities of light can move you through different dimensions when our senses are withdrawn from the third dimension and we look inward.

When the brain and our defenses to survive drop away following death the intense emotions flare up like fear, grief, anger, envy or greed. The individual can be in a swirl of emotion and unable to concentrate or find balance, or stability.

Counselors can describe the problems or issues to the soul and give options for dealing with them. Healthier souls will choose one of the options. Unhealthy souls may deny there are problems and refuse treatment. Just as they did when they had a body, how surprising. If that denial is strong enough the counselors may determine that the individual cannot be helped by them and the soul will be returned to their earlier state of wandering the gray world. The souls that appear open to learning, growth, healing and restoration are helped in an atmosphere of support, growth and nurturing.

**

The pathways that allow your body to function are CHEMICAL and ELECTRICAL; the pathways are the electrical circuitry of the human biology. We usually think of an electrical circuit as a loop of an electrical conductor. However, the electrical circuits in our biology are chemical and they conduct electricity and generate CURRENTS within the body. Our body changes the chemical structure and this circuitry every time we feel an *emotion or have a thought.* Every time we challenge ourselves we create new synaptic pathways. The creation of new pathways is what opens us up to receive communication through our soul. Now that the body is being rewired, creating new pathways will be a much easier process.

The increase of energy is overwhelming the BRAIN. It does not want to be RESTRICTED to only the brain. Are you willing to allow the spiritual energy to enter the entire body? It is perfectly fine and rather desirable to allow the new energy to flow in through ALL PARTS of your body that is how the energy *wants* to come into you.

Many humans at this time are coping with a degree of mental unbalance because of the large amounts of spiritual energy being sent to the earth. There is a large increase of awareness being sent to the entire planet.

✷✷✷

The Indigos, crystals and rainbow children are here to teach us how to be multidimensional. Our reality is nothing but a perception, an illusion. The time has come to look at a much larger picture of who and what we are. Look at things in a new way. This is easier to do when you are in a state of multidimensionality.

The rewiring of our brain will help us become aware of how we are all connected. And as the veil thins everyone will realize they have never been alone, they have an entourage.

All of humanity is raising the collective vibration and as that happens the magnetic structure of Earth changes and vibrates higher.

✷✷✷

CHAPTER 5

BEING A CREATOR

When we say "I AM" we are using our creatorship attribute, our divinity.

The energy of life is flowing through us constantly.

When your energy feels depleted is it because you have used it up clinging to your point of view. Let go of your point of view and return to your divine self, your energy then returns.

When we were in the first creation "All That Is" we had certain creative powers and abilities. Our creative powers and abilities were somewhat limited then.

Our creative powers and abilities are HIDDEN from us in duality.

Our creative abilities and powers in the new energy are **expansive** and almost *unlimited*. In New Energy we replace thinking or philosophy with doing or our CREATIVITY. Creativity will be our new driving force and passion. Do you feel your creative juices flowing and welling up inside you?

Creativity needs our human stimulation to blossom. It asks each day what you choose to create. Allow yourself to experience your creatorship. Potentials for creating are all around you waiting to be invited into the third dimension and your divine human life.

Avoid structuring your creations, soul wants them to be free to expand and have their own meaning and evolution, their own life and identity. That is what true creator energy is all about. It is NOT about owning and controlling. Owning and controlling is all about fear. When the human wants to own and control someone or something the motivation, overtly or covertly, is the human having an emotional issue.

The human needs to work with the emotional issues FIRST, before they can be a compassionate creator. I believe the devil and satan had owning and controlling issues they failed to address appropriately.

Well would you consider an owning and controlling individual able to be a compassionate entity? I think not, there are definitely abuse issues from their childhood or very earliest days to be addressed first.

And what entity have you met that was owning and controlling that could see the BIG picture with any clarity. Dah!

How many times have you enjoyed being "a thing" someone owned or controlled?

And who enjoys playing or creating with them anyway. It is way too challenging to find "the gift ."

To be the creator you will need to severe your romance with **victimhood**, *judgment* or HATE, especially of yourself. If you don't love you why would your creation want to be with you. When you dwell in the lower vibrations of fear, hate, vengeance, judgment, victimhood, addiction or depression taking ninety to seventy percent of your energy, there is no passion left to create something new or different for yourself or another.

"I AM" *summons creation* you are declaring a **fact**.

I AM happy and abundant, another DECLARATION.

You solve future issues by going into NOW time, that is the way of soul.

Humans are the ones that turned the *VOID into REALITY.*

To pull that off we went into the void and CREATED based on *our thoughts* of what **would be in the future.**

The vibrations from our thoughts created PATHWAYS for our future to be manifested. We were setting the templates for future creating. We have operated this way ever since we first arrived on earth. We were bound by memories of our past (karmic) energy and we also needed to balance them out in the future. We created the future by projecting ourselves into the future and rebalancing energy that got distorted from some of our chosen experiences.

When you spend too much time drinking ale or being a porn star you might not of gained as much wisdom as you would have being a compassionate friend or pruning trees.

Most *humans on Earth create* UNCONSCIOUSLY.

Not you of course. The one next to you and me.

Duality and opposition was encoded in our DNA. Our 90%er set up that vibrational FRICTION on purpose for us because that was the experience we were after to increase our understanding, experience and wisdom. Generally speaking we made the ratio of energy in duality one third to two thirds in either direction.

Lifetimes based two thirds in **darkness** and one third in light.

Lifetimes based two thirds in positive and one third in **negativity.**

Encoded in our DNA loops. This was done intentionally for us to be sure we had an opportunity to experience everything we wanted to experience. Both sides of the coin or issue.

In the new energy there is NO LONGER a need for this friction and our balance is slowly being brought back to one-ness, with the opposing aspects incorporated into the one. The evil twin combined with the good twin. Our DNA loops will *begin working together again* and stop opposing each other to get the job done. As they do that it will help to heal all of our past scars by allowing us to own what we have found objectionable in ourselves. Melded DNA will mend our wounds physically and emotionally when we live in the divine NOW moment.

Melded DNA will come from the perspective of our soul, the 90%er. That part of us does not have the intense emotional reactions that our human part has. The 10%er is unable to see beyond their own limited reality and suffering, remember that is how our DNA was structured.

OLD ENERGY: Our creative powers and abilities are hidden from us in duality. Our DNA was encoded with opposition. We setup this vibrational FRICTION on purpose to increase our spiritual wisdom and understanding. Generally speaking we made the ratio of energy in duality one third to two thirds. Our future had been created by us living in our thoughts of what tomorrow would bring and that was appropriate in duality.

NEW ENERGY: Our creative powers and abilities in the new energy are expansive and almost unlimited. Our opposing DNA loops will be melded and working together again as our 90% and 10% start to combine. That will heal the past scars and wounds within all our bodies, seen and unseen when we live in the divine NOW moment. FUTURE REALITY is an **assimilation** of awareness from **ALL** the **HUMANS** and their vibrational frequencies.

Our future had been created by us living in our thoughts of what tomorrow would bring and that was appropriate. This will continue to be appropriate for many on the earth not ready yet to move into new energy. Those living in duality will balance out those moving into the new energy it is all a matter of physics we cannot all do the same thing at the same time. That would unbalance the lot of us.

FUTURE REALITY is an **assimilation** of awareness from **ALL** the **HUMANS** and their vibrational frequencies. A rather large math problem which would make my head hurt to work out.

Fears and concerns you might be having currently could easily have their origin from when we were in the original creation in the first circle. At that time our BUILD UP OF FEARS gave us enough energy to help eject us out of the original first circle so we could experience on God's behalf. The many experiences we have had and continue to have allowed God to know herself.

For those moving into the new energy the fears we are experiencing now could easily be a combination of our OLD fears being **restimulated** and our current FEARS of CHANGE coming into our awareness. That could be allot of fears feeding off each other.

The fears come forth because they WANT RESOLUTION and they want to clear up ANY ISSUES preventing our movement forward. The fears want to know things, knowing calms fears. Often our energy will easily get stuck. I have gone to the trouble of explaining what is happening so the brain understands. The brain needs to remain calm.

Remember we are powerful and can easily create what ever we might need in the now moment. So hoarding anything including piles of money to feel safe is an illusion of safety. When you wrap something in fear you will get back what you put out. *More fear* that there will not be ENOUGH or enough money for your human self to feel safe.

As we **become creators in the new energy** we will learn the importance of living in the divine NOW moment.

NOW has **no judgments.**

NOW is a quiet place where you can feel love washing through or over your entire being. NOW can last for a second or hours. In the NOW we have **NO needs or wants.**

In the divine NOW moment there is a new vibration emanating out from within you ATTRACTING ALL APPROPRIATE things to you.

A creator has to spend considerable time dealing with and sorting out their "issues" before they create. When you have issues you do not understand or feelings you have avoided feeling. You will also AVOID, *twist* or **deny** "feeling information" coming to you from other dimensions.

Creators ESPECIALLY need to resolve and move past their "old issues" from this lifetime and all their past lives with *resolution.* Avoidance doesn't work and it never has, avoidance delays. A creator with unresolved issues will wind up acting them out in their life and creations.

Issues LIKE: *FEAR*, questions and DOUBTS you have about yourself, your competence, your skills and compassion will distort or cripple and most likely, just stop your creation. Having your creation questioned and stopped will prove pretty frustrating and possibly painful to you, THE HUMAN.

We are to be true to our *heart desires* and not a slave to our brain or the bottom line. How are YOU doing with the shift from your overworked brain and opening your heart working with your divine intelligence doing what you want to do with the support and help of your soul?

Consider yourself as having been created by YOUR OWN **creator self.** You are the parent of yourself.

Humans exist outside of the circle of All That Is.

Our soul NO LONGER knows the outcome of what we might do or create.

God doesn't have an agenda or even care what we create. God wants us to enjoy ourselves. So how much practice do you have at having a good time? Just as I thought—not much.

Another human or ANY other ENTITY not even an angel for that matter, **can** create on YOUR BEHALF. We must do ALL OUR CREATING **on our own!** NO HELP ALLOWED.

Oh please, please, please, will not work any more. But, other entities, quantum physics and other humans will join in once we get the ball rolling.

We are experiencing quantum changes at the VERY CORE of our being; our *emotions*, OUR BIOLOGY and our THINKING, the very way we HANDLE everything in our life is changing. We are leaving opposition and moving into unity. Moving from drama to compassion and creativity.

Enjoy the new energies coming into you they will help force out your old baggage creating a lighter you. This process is grander than what we went through in Alt (Atlantis) and Mu (Lemuria). The process is so easy one might have difficulty accepting it. The change can be so subtle and yet profound you might need another to point out the changes happening in you.

And to those that have a pattern of purposely sabotaging themselves to make simple things ever so much more difficult, when you believe it needs to be difficult, you will create that for yourself. Stop doing that if you are ready to, you are wasting your energy silly human.

New energy is fast and efficient it helps you release your struggles.

OLD ENERGY: Creating became a battle of outsmarting and outwitting the competition you told yourself to stuff your doubts and fears, be strong and positive be upbeat. Stiff upper lip and all that.

NEW ENERGY: Though the creator feels fear and self doubt they understand those emotions are true and present. These energies do not need to be considered **negative** they can work with you and for your creations.

FEAR is energy, have some ice cream with it and talk. Feel the fear to see if it is behaving the way it always has in your life? What is new with your fear, has it changed its outfit? Is it any easier to hang with than before. Has it learned anything new that you can use.

Uncertainty is just energy consider it one of "your people" and ask questions of your uncertainty. Clarify exactly who and what you are uncertain about.

You are not uncertain about you are you?

No need to convert your fears or uncertainties just REC-OGNIZE them and invite them into your creation by winning them over to your side. Get their feed back. Catch a new perspective and look at things in a whole new way. You are the one guiding and directing this operation so have fun with the variety of energies you brought into your creation. Get their support and help.

Accept *all* things AS THEY ARE.

This means first and foremost ACCEPT all of yourself as you are.

ALL the parts of **yourself** you have hidden from yourself. There might be a layer or layers of you that will need a great deal of compassion, love and attention **FROM YOU** in order for you to own and feel them enough to be released. When you are UN-ABLE to own and feel those parts they will CONTINUE to keep a barrier between the human and the divine self.

***

DENIAL

Today's example of denial is:
Generally a person coming from an abusive childhood might remember they were abused but are THRILLED that they have lost touch with how painful that felt to them as a child. To get through their childhood it was wise for them to separate out their feelings from the events that took place. They needed to shut down their feelings of BETRAYAL or the frustration, of being told they were **wrong** or **crazy** and of having no control of what happened to their body OR FEELINGS because they were smaller and weaker than the abuser, most likely a family member or two or three.

Full connection with your divine self would be impeded by your **not** FEELING or OWNING the pain you felt as a child or actually anytime in your life. I find it a MOST AMAZING thing that in the new energy this process of reconnecting what happened to us and putting the feelings of the event together again does not need to be a long drawn out process as it always has been.

The reconnection has been made easier by the unseen world.

You might not need to experience the abandonment and suffering for more than a few hours or a day. Invisible realm wants you to be **conscious of how much it pained you** to be treated that way because that will increase your compassion and

SPIRITUAL wisdom. You can't have too much of compassion or spiritual wisdom, can you?

When you have trouble tapping into that pain the invisible realm stands ready and able to help you. Ask them to show you an incident that will restore your feelings TO YOU about a certain event in your past. Allow the feelings to come in, if you push them away they will go away.

When you are feeling braver or more courageous and ready enough to experience the pain ask the invisible realm again to help you feel what you used to feel in a given situation or block of time in your life. If you are alive now you have already gone through the pain at least once and lived. Reliving it one more time will not prove fatal. I promise!

When you have pain or suffering and you do not remember the origin of why, ask the invisible realm to show you the incident that created those feelings. They are happy to share that information with you. I highly recommend you go back to the earliest incident because understanding the earliest incident will release all the ones that happened after that.

So if you only remember the pain or only the event the invisible realm will supply the missing parts for you. All you need do is ask them. Please own what happened, do not judge it. Be aware and gain the spiritual knowledge from your experience.

The other example for today: You were THE ABUSER.

You need to own that and FEEL it. I don't believe there are abusers who have not been abused first. Odds are huge that you did what was done to you so you could gain the spiritual wisdom. And no I do not know WHO started this chain of abuse and you know it does not really matter anymore. It is just the way of things.

The class bully always has at least one parent that bullies them and teaches the child separation, bigotry, and misuse of personal power.

Where does one learn it is ACCEPTABLE to hurt others? At home of course. It is just the way of things, round and round are you strong enough to stop THE CYCLE of abuse?

What you NEED to feel is **how it felt** for YOU to **abuse someone** the way you were abused. What was your conscious choice BEFORE you abused and own that feeling and belief. What belief made you feel entitled to abuse? Just own it! No judging YOU just own the feeling.

Then you will need to FEEL and have COMPASSION for your personal abuse that made you feel entitled to abuse others. Feel how it felt to be abused and totally powerless to do anything about it. Did you judge yourself as a looser and carry that judgment forward in your life? Do you think if you were sweeter or smarter or meaner it wouldn't of happened—WRONG !!! You set it up to increase your spiritual wisdom. So have you gained the wisdom?

Abuse HAS NOTHING to do with you and EVERY-THING to do with your abusers NUTTY thoughts and justifications. If you are an adult abuser to your spouse you are probably just doing what was done to you as a child and the abuse will continue with your child. How cool is all that.

It is just the way of things until someone is compassionate enough to stop it!

If we had specific and vivid recall of all we did in the past it would overwhelm us. It is not necessary to know how many times we repeated the same pattern over and over again.

Own that it happened and recycle it all into something useful.

We are ALSO healing the past of our family bloodline. And have been doing that since before we ever came to Earth. WE are the designated "ascendee" for all our other lifetimes. We are the top life and in control of all the other lifetimes we are living concurrently.

Humans are now birthing a new type of divinity NEVER seen in all of the second creation. Our angelic relatives are watching us and want to know ALL ABOUT WHAT WE ARE DOING, and how we are doing it. I think they are a tad jealous of ALL our wonderfulness.

※※※

Accept *all* things AS THEY ARE.

To be divine and compassionate we need to accept things JUST EXACTLY as they are.

Look at the unity, at the ecosystem of everything and everyone on earth. All the small bits that fit into the whole creation are all interdependent on each other. All the parts and the way things are interconnected together are what you need to accept JUST as they are. Even the homeless person is where they want to be, honor their path if you want to show your compassion.

Perhaps you can become aware of energy and relationships you never have seen before and they would gently ask you, "Please do not interfere with MY process" I AM ON MY OWN PATH AND IT IS NOT YOUR path! Please honor that. It is just the way of things.

Things are EXACTLY as they ought to be.

This is so very hard for us to accept gracefully. We have spent so much time and energy in comparing and finding fault with ourselves and others. And then trying to fix them. Accepting all things as they are will take OUR VERY CONSCIOUS awareness and discipline to stop those kind of thoughts and feelings from running around in our head and OUT our mouth.

Hopefully you have already discovered that your behavior patterns OF FIXING AND CONTROLLING are tiresome, laborious, frustrating and totally nonproductive to a creator. And EXCEEDINGLY irritating to everyone else you try to "fix".

YES, I agree sometimes people ask for help and if you think they mean it by all means give them your HELP.

When you are holding onto to belief systems and concepts that served you at one time and are not serving you now it will be DIFFICULT to be a creator in the new energy. As you become aware of and break through your mass consciousness programing you will gain new understanding about the illusion we are in and how controlling and limited THEY ARE. Certainly not at all conducive to exercising your creator abilities and skill in a smooth flowing manner.

When a human or any entity gets sucked into drama they expend there creator energy and creativity IN THE DRAMA leaving no juice left to create with. My point is, that it is either / or. Partaking in drama, making a stage production of one of your feelings depletes you. You can enjoy "drama" or "create" it is your choice. Rejecting drama does not mean you stop feeling. You will still feel the full range of emotions. Feeling your emotions does not deplete you.

We are straddling two worlds at this time so when you feel the third dimension emotions and drama coming on you, the divine part of you can simply accept and observe them. In accepting and honoring your human self you will come to know your divine self better the two are rather different and complementary.

As you and your soul work in concert you will be moving to higher dimensions of vibration where the negative low vibrating emotions drop away from you as your DNA comes into unity and more of your soul comes through you. The amount of compassion you feel for others will start increasing and the desire to control everyone else's life goes away, must be a low vibration.

It is so wonderful to feel NO OBLIGATION to run everyone else's life.

There is certainly periods of going back and forth between third dimension and all the other dimensions. When the biology gets ill or is cleansing, it vibrates lower you might fall out of the cosmic flow of your soul for a bit. When the biology is out of balance you vibrate lower and become more prone to lower vibrating issues like fear confusion and doubt.

Living in the divine NOW moment is a richer fuller higher vibrating experience.

As a creator you will not live in the **past** or the FUTURE. You will live in the now moment which includes the past and the future all at the same time. In the divine moment the healing process is exponentially faster, aging is greatly slowed and we decide when we want to separate from the biology.

Breathe deeply within your being from the top of the head all the way through the body down to your toes. Breathe in deeply allowing your divine energy that resides within you to come forth. Allow the now moment in every cell. Honor and love yourself. Our new relationship with our soul and divinity is accomplished through breathing. The breathe will feed and nurture the divinity within.

Breathe in abundance it is coming from within you. Allow all things to manifest in your life. Paying your bills breathe in ABUNDANCE. Relationship problems breathe in *balanced rela-*

tionships. Breathe in your own self worth and ACCEPTANCE, breathe it in deeply.

The feeling of loneliness is replaced with love, fullness and a unity at the core level of your being.

When in doubt breathe.

Even those without bodies breathe to move their stuck energy and integrate the new or difficult.

On your path to integrating new energy it is *not possible* to **drag** along your past it is a quantum physics thing.

You cannot apply the new on top of the old.

The old needs releasing to allow the new to move in.

Breathe it in, OWN IT and FEEL IT then transmute and bless it. Then the past becomes just a memory without strong emotions attached to it. Your old self has been leaving you bit by bit being replaced by your new divine self, your soul.

***

VIBRATION

Our music IS vibration. On the other side of the veil they do not usually call vibration music. On the other side they play with vibrations created from within them. They create tonal or vibrational balances and harmonies, alone or in groups. Their music is beautiful, entertaining and fun to them. I can't give you a first hand account I just do not remember.

We hear their vibrations as a purring when they come into our space. yes like the noise that cat makes. The vibrational balances and harmonies from the other side do not have the depth and soul of the music we create here on earth. The other side greatly enjoys our music. Our vibrations literally tell the stories of our dramatic lifetimes, experiences and loves, the stories of us on earth and all our pathos through the ages.

Music helps **facilitate cell changes** in our bodies.

Our cells prefer the softer more pleasing music to change in.

The crystals in our computers are what make up the heart of the computer. Silicone (crystal) diodes or semiconductors are the foundation of all computers. The semiconductors are no different than the crystals we keep around the home or carry with us. Crystal has the highest vibration of the mineral kingdom and is as alive as we are. Crystals are living breathing entities that hold vibration and since they make up the very heart of your computers it could easily be said the computers are alive. They too are going through an evolutionary process as a result of our evolution.

Alternating current is a man-made form of electricity and does not exist in nature so, it is not fully understood by those of Crystal vibration. The Crystal Children are challenged by alternating current and can easily burn out electrical devices with normal usage. This is because the crystal child has no frame of reference with alternating current, they naturally reflect the current back, amplifying it back to the device it came from, the devices find the over stimulating and tend to blow up a lot around these children.

The Crystal Children's eyes can lock onto yours and it feels like a high level being is scanning you. Their eyes hypnotize adults. They are merely **gathering information** about humans and the planet they are on. They are sending out messages of LOVE, *understanding* and **wisdom**. Their high level spiritual frequencies and their ego-free personalities indicate that they're very spiritually evolved. They have magnetic personalities.

Crystal Children are here to teach us about love and save us from ourselves. THAT is no small task.

Just having a crystal child seems to awaken latent psychic abilities in their parents. They might not know how to communicate verbally very well. Many parents say their children created their own form of sign language with each other and some communicate through drawings.

Crystal Children are born psychic, and do not let others talk them out of it. They see angels and spirit guides and are mind readers. They become incredibly focused as if in a trance.

They rely on their intuition to discern the truth about people and situations. They are constantly scanning their surroundings. Absorbing to many negative energies can adversely affect them. *Crystals are unable to go into DENIAL*. Sometimes they will act out the anger or frustration they feel from others. They have so much love in their hearts that their presence has a healing effect. They direct energy with their hands, thoughts and effect profound healing.

The crystal is poised to retain their spiritual, psychics gifts into adulthood thanks to supportive parents and grandparents. Crystals are visual, right brained dominant, visual instead of language based. They need to have things explained not forced. They want you to pay attention and never LIE or *bend the truth* and you need to **keep your word**.

Whales are living portions of the crystalline grid. They contain the "history of Earth", within them, they coordinate and cooperate with the grid. Dolphins are their cousins and support group. Whales dolphins, amphibians, birds, and insects all navigate to breeding ground or migration every year via the magnetic grid/ ley lines. Since it changed so much, so quickly the animals haven't adjusted and are confused that is why some have beached themselves.

The energy around us is called the cosmic lattice.

Back to the hardened mineral.

Crystals store frequencies and frequencies ARE a language. Frequencies arranged in the proper manner, numbers and cycles are the language our souls use.

The Cave of Creation is a real cave in the third dimension with physical crystalline energy in the form of many crystals in the cave. The cave is shielded from detection those not spiritually awakened would think it a beautiful cave of crystals but not be able to sense what was present. The Akashic Records are the master storage of everything that happened on earth. Our DNA is the storage of current events happening. The current happenings we can take out to reevaluate or enhance our spiritual wisdom.

We have the history of our planet stored in the Crystalline structure of the planet. The Crystalline Grid and Akashic Records on the planet are being rewritten currently and the result will be that *human consciousness will be changed also.* The facts will not change all our wars, conquerors, and the many civilizations and what you had for breakfast today will stay the same. But we can change ALL of the DNA history AROUND the past that is alive today, like your spiritual awareness.

You still have time to decide you hated or loved what you ate for breakfast today, if you wish.

When we come up with a new perspective of the events in our lives THAT CAN alter our DNA information. You could realize it was not breakfast you hated it was the person you were eating with that turned your stomach. Then you and your DNA will stop reacting emotionally and dramatically to eating breakfast and any other layers of history you have with breakfast.

We are rewriting the history of the living grid of human consciousness at this time. The rewrite changes our views on the meaning and definition of what has happened inside of us, our many thoughts and emotional reactions to what has happened.

Looking at events in a new way can increase our spiritual wisdom. Was the event in your life a DRAMA or a LESSON or were you so overwhelmed by stimuli that you could not make sense of what you experienced at all. Were the events part of a greater plan, chaos or an unforeseen consequence. Two people experiencing the same event can have opposite reactions, anger or hatred or a desire to help and rebuild or destroy.

How did your behavior make you feel, proud or humiliated. Could your experience be a model of what to embrace or turn away from, has there been a call to action or a knowingness happening.

Was your reaction revenge or a solution?

We are creatures of interdimensionalality. During our life on earth we have had VERY LIMITED awareness of everything else going on all around us.

As our awareness increases we want to rewrite what happened on earth with a much LARGER awareness than humans have ever had before. Look at the much larger picture with NEW clarity and understanding.

Grace comes from WITHIN us.

Humor is the only thing that passes untouched to us from the other side of the veil because humor begets JOY. They want us to have joy.

I know, it feels like being a human is to have all the joy squeezed right out of you.

The egg shaped layer immediately around our body is called the auric field. This field is **filling up or illuminating** waiting for us to bring it into ourselves, breathe it in now. When it is in us we than RADIATE the illumination out. You will need to give the illumination time to anchor itself in you so continue to work on breathing that helps anchor it.

The unity and balance begins *within the human*. The unity for this world begins with you, be the example to all the other humans.

Earth is a pilot project for the future of certain parts of the universe.

We are the unconscious creators. In the new energy we always express outwardly in vibration that can grow, waves and waves of love go out from within us they are us. As our waves go out they *change the vibration* in things, people and human consciousness.

SPIRITUAL BALANCE is present in these waves moving out. Purity, completeness and a state of perfection are also sent out in those waves. It is up to the recipient of this energy to decide what they want to do with it.

Doing nothing is a valid choice.

The creator will start a creation and then adds their pure love and passion to it when we create in higher vibrations. The waves the creator sends out brings back everything needed for creating in a timely and appropriate manner.

Here is the RUB when you don't work with the energy as it comes to you it will leave. The energy may come in the form of a person, object, thought, event or even the challenge itself may go away.

Express your emotions of anger and pain or joy, work with EXACTLY what shows up! Do not demand that what shows up be different, conforming to your preconceived notion.

Yes you need to be rather flexible.

Sometimes there is NOTHING that shows up, that is a good time to check the unseen world's time line, see if you are following it. When there is nothing, **pain** or *surprise* own and create with THAT. For it is all part of the SURPRISE in the package. Embrace the moment and discover the hidden parts.

Any fears of doing things wrong are UNFOUNDED and there is NO way to study HOW TO DO things right. We are making it up as we go.

You are functioning in the now moment.

When YOU worry you are not trusting your divinity or your human self. Worry alters and lowers the vibrations you send out. Worry is a form of *fear giving you* a **lower level** of what you are in process of creating.

This has been the way of it and it has been such a very long time since we proactively created. Shame and guilt are associate with what we created proactively in the past. We have trouble trusting ourselves now fear, panic and anxiety come in when we start creating. Those feelings are appropriate and natural energies to have at this time, *embrace them*.

Remember battling anything INCREASES **its** power.

Sit with the various forms of fear energy you have. See what it has to say.

Ask YOUR FEAR what it wants to do? Be released, transmuted or incorporated into your project.

This spiritual journey is an individual journey. Yet all of the angelic families are taking this journey as a unit now. Looking outside of yourself to fill any void you feel in yourself or distracting yourself with another **person** or *project* will slow your journey up in direct proportion to the time you spend avoiding yourself. Maybe you chose to go slowly.

In the first circle, All That Is, we did not have free choice. Our free will in the second circle enabled us to create new places and have thoughts and emotions of any kind that struck our fancy. Free will was a mind blowing new toy for us. We created stars and planets and new energies or battled with other entities. With this new toy of free will also came our many experiences with grief, hardship and suffering along with our perceived loss of oneness.

With free will we went to the lowest of the low, depression and suffering. We went to the highest of the high wonderful places of love and sharing and compassion in the creation of light.

In order to step into DIVINE WILL we need to release our **free will** first. One side must be released before the other side can be experienced. When you step into divine will, releasing free will, things expand **rapidly.**

With the NOW moment comes the *answers and solutions,* along with a much broader picture. We see and experience through the soul and cosmic intelligence. In the now moment we know exactly what to do. First you must step into DIVINE WILL which is so much grander, more complete and more fulfilling than FREE WILL.

Our divine self will not allow us to create inappropriately.

God defies explanation from the brain.

Let go of your old notion of God and embrace life.

Jesus wanted us to realize that each one of us can do exactly what he did! *Our divinity* has NO VOICE or WORDS. Our divinity is a feeling and a **knowingness** a warmth and depth. Jesus was / is *a collective of our energy* he does not have a soul but the energy is very real. The energy of Jesus is changing because we are different and changing.

There is NO NEED for us to be **saved from anything.**

FEELING from the heart is a natural gift from our soul. We have to work HARD to close our heart down.

Childhood abuse does close the heart down pretty nicely. If that was your experience it is your job to be brave enough to **feel again and open up your heart** so you and soul can open up communication. That might not be easy and you might need some help with that.

TO OPEN UP THE HEART allow yourself TO FEEL and breathe.

Light and dark are the same energy embrace them both.

Know that in every part of darkness there is light.

There is no sin only the rules and laws that were created by humans to torment other humans. It is HUMANS that call *certain behaviors* SINFUL, not God. You will not find your *soul through pain* all you find that way is more pain. Suffering goes when YOU CHOOSE to release it.

Release the perception of painfulness, that is a value judgment.

Look at your experience from another point of view, a much larger perspective. Look closely at the individual inflicting the experience you are having, are YOU out of control or dissociated? ARE YOU?

Is there anything you can do to help YOU stop doing what you are doing. Can you show yourself compassion and understanding?

When you or another are dissociated (you can tell by the glazed look in the eyes) get in their face and command that they come up to present time! Keep doing that until they do come up to present time.

LIVING OUTSIDE the NOW moment you loose your feelings.

To enhance your creatorship stop grabbing things and bringing them to you. Stop demanding what you want there is no need to do that. The right things are there as you need them. LET what you want COME TO YOU.

Are you feeling what I am saying.

Wait and soul brings the best probabilities FOR YOU to pick from. No need for you to push and shove for what the human wants. As you move from free will into divine will the human needs to make the best of what soul presents. Be the grateful child all 10% of you. Forcing or demanding any other option can get VERY frustrating, I promise.

OLD ENERGY: Instructors set down rules and conditions as defined in lesson plans. Have tests on what was learned. Imagination has been ignored and been given a bad name. MIRACLES are DRAMA. Visualization is old and from the brain NOT creative.

NEW ENERGY: Instructors of spiritual understanding need to know it can be done. Imagination is the intelligence of the new energy. In oneness there are no opposing forces. Imagination is used to create with.

IMAGINATION is the intelligence of the new energy and is used by the creator to create with. There is no right or wrong. Your imagination can MOVE into and *through* all the DIMENSIONS and can solve challenges. Imagination is in your tool kit and use of the imagination is how we explore all our available probabilities so we can pick which ones we want to expand and develop. Integrate compassion into your being and your imagination goes off to see what is going on everywhere, it senses the many layers that surround you. Imagination is in a NEW TYPE of FLOW and when you send out for people or supplies they come to you.

✿✿✿

IMAGINATION

There is no right or wrong and your imagination wants to be allowed to come to life NOW and express itself. Let yourself know you are in a safe place and now is the right time to AL-

LOW your imagination to come forward and be embraced and integrated with the rest of yourself.

Your imagination can MOVE into and *through* all the DIMENSIONS.

Imagination can solve challenges. Imagination has been given a bad reputation IN OLD ENERGY and called a time waster. Not any longer.

Imagination has largely been ignored and put down but it is one of the good guys. Let your imagination COME to you. Use of the imagination is the most efficient ways to explore all our available probabilities, we can pick which ones we want to *expand and develop.*

Visualization is old and NOT creative it's a form of focusing the mind.

INTEGRATE COMPASSION into your being and your imagination goes off to see what is going on everywhere. Your imagination senses the many layers that surround you. Imagination is in a NEW TYPE of FLOW and when you send out for people or supplies they come to you.

Creating gold is a very limited potential.

Notice when we expand in the new energy the old energy of opposition tries to pull you back to the old ways. You push forward and it pulls back. Fight opposition and you play with OLD energy.

Let opposition pass *through your embrace.*

<u>EMBRACE</u> is to hold tenderly. When you choose opposition your divinity will wait for your embrace. The embrace is the way your divinity will join you. If you do not embrace life you will not have potentials. Embrace but do not strangle your experience or get bogged down with the details.

***

Can you stop making life difficult or sabotaging yourself?
Can you tenderly embrace life and yourself.

The IMAGINATION REALM is also a meeting place for angels and all other entities without bodies including the earth bound. Humans frequently go there while asleep. The imagination realm is a busy place. In the imagination realm, the fourth dimension they do not speak with words they use angel speak, packets of information are exchanged with the divas, fairies or your pets even. Intuition and inner knowingness is used. Some entities might "play" with you while you are there because they understand it is real and humans DO NOT know it is real.

Children go to the imagination realm and it can be fearful to them.

We go to the imagination realm to pick a potential and then allow it to materialize in the third dimension. Bring the potential you felt in the imagination realm into matter in the third dimension. At first release the old beliefs and the way you think things OUGHT TO BE. Observe everything with NO rules or methods.

The times we try to create and nothing happens we have fallen back on the old energy tools like ESP or psychic power which is pushed from the brain. Forcing the brain is very exhausting and not too expansive.

We create in the new energy from the heart in concert with our divine self. Use feeling and your divine knowingness.

The imagination realm is changing because of the new energy.

There are now two realms. The ghosts and demons are not comfortable in the new higher vibrating energy. The new imagination realm is running parallel to the old fourth dimension realm. Allow the new fourth dimension to come into your life. All answers in the new energy are here and it is a safe place. If you want to be sure you are in the right place FEEL it. Is there freedom and no rules or laws? The new energy imagination realm is full, expressive, expansive and open.

Delusion does not fit or feel appropriate in your life. Delusions are a temporary distractions that can be fearful, restrictive and controlling.

There is also old and new energy passions.

OLD ENERGY: Passion was based on duality and very limited. The imagination realm could be uncomfortable—they let ANYONE in.

NEW ENERGY: Passion is expansive and open to many new realms, IT IS LOVE EXPRESSED. Passion is fuel. The imagination realm is a higher vibration and safer because only those with compassion and love can "hang."

<u>PASSION</u> is love expressed, expansive and open to all the many new realms. Passion is fuel. If you are not so sure what to do sit in a quiet moment and feel what passion has to say. The answer of knowingness will come to you. When we attempt to control new energy passion with old human ways *it will hurt us.*

***

PASSION IS LOVE EXPRESSED

When you are not so sure what your passion or desire is, or what you should do, sit in a quiet moment or twelve and feel your "passions wish." The answer will come to you. You will get an answer of knowingness. Our passion is fuel to express our love within. When we attempt to control or direct our passion with our old energy ways, it will hurt us.

Divine balance comes from within you along with all the wisdom you have gained from your past experiences and keep gaining or remembering in the now moment.

The New Creators are the ones who remained here on earth in body and are able to call upon their divinity. They are creating, and will create a new environment, different science, expanded math and energy for themselves that will affect and help others who are wanting to evolve or become creators.

As we become creators from the heart (our 90%er) we will have increased periods of feeling balanced. Serenity will be difficult for the rest of the creators life, but a peaceful balance will be appropriate. We are gaining a deeper understanding of balanced love.

The answers we seek are being found in different locations AND the location of answers is continually changing. When we are in the NOW moment there will be solutions that have never been available to us before. **Solutions** could not make their way through our FREE WILL and *duality*. In the NOW moment the primary focus is NOT on the individual but a compassion and understanding for all coming from the soul. Moving into now or divinity will *releases our free will* as we once again make a connection with our soul in oneness.

Our CIRCLE of completion is **NOW** at hand.

Staying in the now moment we move into acceptance and embracing our divinity, that We Are God Also. Being the creator we start to expand in all directions. We expand by creating and living life for the sake of PURE ENJOYMENT. Do you hear that ENJOYMENT!!!

Soul at play is your divine intelligence.

Playing and creating with all the new potentials coming in. The concepts of happiness and passion, duty, service etc…Have a different definitions than they did in old energy. In new energy there is a freedom and grace so LET IT FLOW. After creating with it release the energy to grow as it wishes.

A HEADS UP:

Each higher vibrational level we raise to will start a new round of physical changes within our biology and some may be physically uncomfortable but not lasting too long. Higher vibrations will increase the sensitivities of our body and all our senses. The increased energy coming in greatly increase our feelings and awareness.

We will start seeing and feeling more and more beyond the obvious.

Accept *all* things AS THEY ARE.

NOW has **no judgments** all is exactly as it should be.

Have no agendas. No conforming to YOUR specifications.

In the NOW, our divinity will have **NO needs or wants**.

When God gives you a nudge, you better do something or he'll give you a shove. Those that are unawakened think they are victims instead of creators.

What potentials have you put in your path to serve you?

***

The law of COMPENSATION

We do NOT RECEIVE in the exact manner and time we choose but the invisible realm works in its own way and time. There is no service lovingly and willingly rendered that ever goes without reward. The reward seldom comes from the source to which the service was given. Be a gracious receiver of what ever you get.

We demonstrate the exact EQUIVALENT of our ability to RECEIVE. There is no limit to compensation. The only limitation is THE ONE WE CREATE through refusal to use what we have or an inability to accept what we are lovingly given.

The law is that—AS WE THINK, SPEAK AND ACT, WE RECEIVE.

Nonresistance has nothing to do with with what a person does. The effects of nonresistance are peace, tranquillity and serenity. Nonresistance IS LOVE and knowing each person Is God Also and deserves our respect and freedom to express themselves in their own unique way.

Nonresistance is a freeing agent it is not passivity or escapism. We need to allow the threads of a circumstance to ease. Then take whatever action is necessary to remove the tangled situation from our life.

Thoughts we have go out past the third dimension.

Our THOUGHTS ARE THINGS . Its quite a responsibility to know that our every thought CREATES. With free will, we have the right to choose how we will think about our experiences and our feelings always follow. With divine will your soul has nonresistance.

You can't hurt another without hurting the self.

Creativity needs human stimulation. Allow yourself to experience your creatorship. Potentials are all around you waiting to be invited into the third dimension and your life.

Soul at play is your divine intelligence.

Solutions could not make their way through our FREE WILL and *duality.*

Stop grabbing things and bringing them to you.

Stop demanding what you want. Soul delivers the right things as you need them. Let it all COME TO YOU. Are you feeling what I am saying. *Wait* and soul brings the best probabilities FOR YOU to pick from. No need for pushing and shoving.

As you move from free will into divine will the human needs to make the best of what soul presents. Be the grateful child all 10% of you.

<u>EMBRACE</u> is to hold tenderly. When you choose opposition your divinity will wait for your embrace. The embrace is the way your divinity will join you. If you do not embrace life you will not have potentials. Embrace but do not strangle your experience or get bogged down with the details.

***

In the NOW moment the primary focus is NOT on the individual but a compassion and understanding for all. Moving into the now moment or our divinity will release our free will as we connect up with our soul in oneness.

The amount we embrace of our *divine self* will be the amount we lose of our **human self.**

Instead of asking for answers, ask for balance.

The creator views life as perfect. You can create by deciding what energy is to be removed. Sometimes it's with the MIND or **real action.** The creator walks in a perfect place, even with a dying child, crime or suffering. Another human's anger, suffering, drama or imbalance never changes the reality that all is in a state of perfection.

The closer you get to perfection the more you remove what is inappropriate in your life. When you start resonating with the perfection within your creation, you get manifestation. The process begins by claiming and acting on your integrity in all areas of your life.

We are in charge of our reality.

The crystal energy started being delivered to earth in 2001 through 2005 and we had a pause in 2006 for us to assimilate it. In 2007 the delivery of crystal energy for our next bit of evolution will be coming and causing change and upheavals as we assimilate more of it. This energy will help humanity balance its energy and move into a higher vibration.

When the sun erupts into a solar flare it sends magnetic energy to the earth changing our magnetic structure slightly with each layer and level, wave of crystal energy.

The sun is a dimensional portal for energy serving our solar system.

As we get closer to the poles of the earth the energy is more conducive to manifesting. The densest consciousness on the planet is at the equator. Some of your most "enlightened" cities are toward the top and bottom of the earth's land masses. Some of the most profound problems are at the equator. It's not an issue of fairness, it is about balance. Everyone who is born in their respective areas actively chose to be there.

Those wanting to be creators need to acknowledge that they, the 10%er and 90%er together, are the highest power in the universe. That no other power can do things to you or defeat you in any way, there is nothing that can affect you unless you allow it to.

The human has **free choice**.

The creator has *divine will*.

Letting it be okay for things to turn out differently than the human wants is a hard one at times. If you can develop the skill of adjusting to a huge human expectation not happening and then alter the human future and desire to be in joy with what soul gives.

"Created equal." means HUMANS are all divine creatures, whose SPIRITUAL abilities are the same. That would be true for the criminal and the oppressors. It's what you do with your spiritual awareness that changes your reality and that of the planet.

At this time the earth is the only planet populated with divine creatures. When we are not human, we are able to see the bigger picture. AND then we can hardly wait to return to the earth and continue this experience and help with this test of energy and vibration.

Duality hides who we really are and the grand plan. The earth providing an unbiased answer to a grand universal question. Where will the energy ultimately settle when the final measurement is made. When we are in our natural eternal state we are part of the planners and creators of the universe. Yes, the earth is a test of energy and vibration.

The final measurement of the earth was to be now and all our prophets said so, they called it the "end times." But the humans changed the vibration high enough to negate the old prophesies.

Did the prophesies of the ages happen?

No they didn't.

The test has been extended.

What happens on earth will eventually affect life in a whole new universe. What we are doing right now is known to all on the other side of the "veil." They are challenging us to keep going and find solutions to the formerly unsolvable and actually discover our divinity.

This has been the reason for all the teaching and support the humans have gotten from the unseen world.

The "bias" of God is love. As we draw into a higher vibration, that very biased cheering section is becoming audible to our cells.

We are creators and creatures of habit.

Seven times we must purposefully try to create a new pattern before it has a chance of taking hold.

***

Now more than ever, we are feeling the compression of time and space. Those things that used to bring great joy are somehow not as nice as they used to be. As we step into a higher vibration *we reach for higher truths.*

Take a daily walk in the interdimensional bubble of love to feel peaceful and loved, that way your cells will be refreshed and refuse to go into drama, anger or worry.

When we say "I AM" we are using our creatorship attribute, our divinity.

When you can take responsibility for the illusion you created for yourself that cancels out any possibility of you being the victim. If you were the victim that is what you wanted.

You absolutely created ALL of what you have.

***

CHAPTER 6

Some other ways of NEW ENERGY

Remember that being human is a game, an illusion, so do your very best to enjoy the experience.

The entire cosmos is getting the new expansive energy and no one human or any other entity, knows exactly how it will work. Earth is the grandest smartest and most advanced planet. We all have ascended into the New Energy like it or not. During this process we will totally reintegrate all of our aspects. The human will become consciously aware of all her aspects or the 90% we have had little awareness of while we are human.

We will arrive at a whole new holistic relationship between ourselves and how our soul and physical body work in unison.

We aren't responsible for creating the soul of other people, but the way we relate to them **is our creation**.

An enemy is *created in your own heart*.

All monsters live in a dark place where humans stuff their **fears**, SHAME and *guilt*. Presently, fear is more clearly heard on earth than love is.

Going inward with our CREATIVE ENERGY rather than outward will create depression in the human. When the human is depressed the soul leaves off supporting the human. Maybe takes a vacation. **The soul waits.**

Repression of energy is the greatest problem on this planet.

BEING God and repressing **anything** will create problems in our *biological and emotional bodies.*

Repression always has caused problems in our biology and emotional bodies and we are becoming even more sensitive to that than ever before. We need to move our creative energy outward. We need to help each other move their creative energy outward rather than inward.

Technology reflects the vibrational state of the *race it serves.*

When technology passes the amount of heart energy generated by the people an imbalance is created. As heart energy rises technology will be pulled up to match the heart. This explains why we have had such huge technological advances in the past fifty years.

In Atlantis we used crystal energy. Now we are using electricity and fossil fuel to run our technologies. The crystal energy we used in Atlantis may return soon because we are in need of alternative energy sources. As long as there is a balance of heart energy and technology it will work well.

The Atlantis energy crystals have remained in the Atlantic Ocean. The crystals have been reactivated through our heart energy opening up. Be aware of and feel that energy as it passes through you. Use the crystal energy to filter through your own heart. Fear will automatically be transmuted into love energy on these crystals. The web of love humans have created and use to connect to each other has been reactivating the green heart energy of the crystals of Atlantis.

Although the green crystals will not be moved from the Atlantic Ocean for some time, energy from them has already begun.

Intelligence is not just from the mind. In this lifetime we are going to see how consciousness transcends the intellectual.

Consciousness "is." The last few years there has been a rapid acceptance of new thought like alternative medicines and lifestyles and especially a growing spirituality. Those humans saying "Hold onto the past" is a way of balancing an energy dynamic. When rapidly evolving consciousness gets caught in the mind it causes clashes.

We are in process of going beyond our old mental limitations which means we need to break down the old so there is room for the new. So there will be many clashes of old and new.

This lifetime we have been developing our relationship with ourselves. Getting to know ourselves and prepare to blend with our soul.

THE STAGES WE HUMANS GO THROUGH

First there is pure survival as we work on improving our human condition.

Secondly we make things bigger and better and more comfortable.

THIRDLY there is still an unrest IN US and we are less happy than we have ever been.

Fourthly, frustrated and unable to find fulfillment we get depressed. When the human is depressed the soul leaves off supporting the human. The soul waits. Sometimes the human keeps searching until they discover spiritual awareness and a desire to know of things beyond the human condition.

Finally the human is wanting to develop a relationship with themselves as a result of their spiritual awakening. Choose love and true spiritual union with your invisible parts over fear.

The human wants to know more about themselves and soul.

First we start developing a relationship with our body which is conflictual because our body has been used against us and gotten in our way frequently. The body gets tired, hungry and cranky and is not as beautiful as we had hoped it would be. The body is high maintenance. There have been car accidents, maybe the body was beat or abused some. Humans are funny they blame the body. The body also prevents us from leaving earth.

The body absorbed most of the abuse and energy imbalances so develop a rapport with the body and all its parts. The body needs a great deal of compassion and you taking responsibility and dominion over your body. Give the body permission to release toxins and the imbalances. Get rid of the old pent up energies through breathing.

Repair of our physical body is much easier than what we have been led to believe it is. We have made things far more difficult than they are. And the brotherhood of light will help heal your auric body. Just ask them.

When you are having a solid relationship with yourself and your soul, life flows much easier and more naturally and abundance is present. The invisible realms definition of abundance not the human definition. When you are listening and not compromising or judging and demanding certain outcomes life can flow rather smoothly.

TO RECAP we go from survival to comfort, a spiritual awareness and ultimately relationship with your total self, the visible and invisible.

We are *gifted* on a spiritual and intuitive level.

We are resistant to the idea that life can be lived with ease. We have caged and restricted ourselves for no good reason. We have shut down large chunks of ourselves. When your own life is fragmented how can you do anything constructive for yourself or another individual?

We are done being stuck or trapped by old contracts.

Each and every day you are with a situation or at work or with a partner, family or friends YOU NEED to make the choice to stay or leave. You need to chose no longer is it a destiny or curse or vow you made eons ago. Embrace who you are or what you do **or release it** and move *it on down the road.* Do not "suffer" with anything or anyone, any longer.

We have such a conflicted relationship with the body. If you would be interested in healing and strengthening your body relationship start breathing into the body and talking to the biology. Breathing into your body convinces the body you are on the same team and want to continue living. True breathing demands being in the present moment and IN your body. Way too many humans are out of their body and not at home.

A reasons for disassociation with our soul and our body is our propensity to compromise over and over until we don't remember who we are anymore. Our childhood taught us to be masters of compromise. We were taught compromise was a good and proper thing to do at home and at school. Revisit and ponder the value of compromising yourself. There is new information and a new perspective, now that we are divinity. Compromise is an illusion created by duality to keep you small and held down and back.

Do not compromise.

Our core beliefs and essence is what we compromise when we try to appease other people or are fearful of being our own I AM. We compromise when we search outside of the self to get our needs met or for the answers.

Compromise is always giving in to the other human and letting them feed on you. Compromise of the self is when you know something and then doubt yourself and hold back.

Breathing opens up consciousness and awareness that will scare many humans, consciousness is NOT what they want more of.

Getting friendly with your body leads to a relationship with the mind and the awareness that it is not the be all end all. Your mind gets put into perspective as a part of you and not all there is. Then the mind looses its power to **disorient** you. Many have never felt their soul because the mind got in the way.

Developing a relationship to the body evolves into developing a relationship with our divinity. A relationship with the body also helps our interdimensional understanding.

As we complete our journey of experiences two behaviors that are prevalent in duality, END!

1. The endless goal setting we have made for ourselves is OVER. You can throw your daily planner away.

2. Our making amends in an effort to balance energy that we made lopsided is OVER, no more karma.

Hold back energy in the new energy and it comes out anyway **explosively** it wants the *joy of expression* and EXPANSION. Compromising yourself will not prevent the joy of expression and expansion. Continue to COOPERATE but do not *compromise your core values.*

Are you DISTRUSTING yourself and fearful of the world outside?

Are you relying on other things or people and the angelic beings?

When you expect others to carry you and distrust yourself that is NOT BEING TRUE to yourself. WHEN WE ARE DISLOYAL TO OURSELVES we brake off parts of us and fragment and split ourselves up depleting our energy which results in disorientation and YOU PRETENDING you don't know who you are anymore. Sever the connection with dependency and doubt. Change those patterns—You Are God Also! Start acting like it. You need to decide if you want to hang on the alter of obligation any longer.

Compromise yourself and your *energy level and life force drops.*

No **SUFFERING** with *anyTHING* or ANYone anymore.

No longer accept struggling and misery on behalf of humanity or even on behalf of yourself. The world does not need a place to dump its problems because it serves NO one. Not those doing the dumping or those doing the accepting of the problems. Someone has to end that cycle. Just say NO!

Question who should we suffer for and who should we suffer with?

Have people in your life more earthbound than you taking your energy? It happens regularly and is not necessarily a bad thing but be aware of it and care for yourself find a little time for you. Not meditation, yoga or that sort of thing. Just time with yourself to flow energy and maintain a higher degree of your radiance and your expansion.

You can also handicap yourself when you ignore what your knowingness tells you. Deciding instead to follow conventional wisdom and disowning your knowledge, compromises you.

KNOWINGNESS or gnost is NOT known to the **brain**. Knowingness comes from other dimensions or realms as your essence does, it is a type of dream or imagination state. Going to that state will allow you to bring that information or essence into the third dimension and after grounding it here it starts transforming itself into an energy that eventually will be understood by the mind. That is where breakthroughs and "ahas" come from.

✳✳✳

When we go to other realms or dimensions we take our **essence** to those places NOT the brain. When we try to remember what we saw or did or experienced the brain has stayed on earth so it will be of no help when you want information from those trips. The challenging part is that you need to go back into your essence for the information at your knowingness level.

Your essence is a type of dream or imagination state on the same level as your knowingness functions. Your essence or imagination states can enable you to bring that information into the third dimension. First you need to ground it in the third dimension, and after grounding it here the information starts transforming itself into an energy that eventually will be understood by the mind. That is where the breakthroughs and the "ahas" come from. We can even bring knowingness, breakthroughs in and "ahas" into the third dimension on behalf of other humans that want or need the information and are sadly trying to squeeze it out of their brain. POOR brain.

The imaginative types of this world go frequently to the crystalline realms to create and that energy does not always respond well when brought into manifest in the third dimension.

Playing in the other realms is more fun than here. There you have instant manifesting. Working hard to manifest in third dimension makes creative types want to stay in the other dimensions. If that is you, consider allowing others to be the actual builders or manifestos. You share your creation with them. There are many people wanting to be the builders the doers of creating. Of course you yourself could get more grounded with deep breathing, get fully present, here and then expand and bring your creation in.

Projecting yourself out of your body is not being expansive and takes a lot of your energy. Get in the now moment and get solidly INTO your body, then while staying in your body bring the dimension in the present moment which conserves your energy.

Bringing your creations to the third dimension will be easier then. That way you can stop creating frustration and impatience in yourself.

✵✵✵

DEBT

Having to earn money is a *distorted* belief system.

Debt is an **illusion** with a great deal of DRAMA and **emotion** that sucks the life right out of you. Abundance flows easily when you are in your passion and not so easy when you are not in your passion. When doing other than your passion, things tend to get taken away.

Debt can represent the extent that you are clinging to past life incidences, possibly trying to reclaim *something you feel you are owed*. The same for childhood abuses you might be trying to reclaim *something you feel you are owed* because of all that was taken.

Money is only one form of debt to consider. Another type of debt or energy you cling to could be WORRY or *guilt* possibly **fear** or shame. Give it some thought and consider working off that debt or owning it and release it in now time. Debt does not enhance one's life. Work on enjoying what you can pay for, borrowing from others is not divine behavior. Sharing is divine.

At times we fear we are going backwards when what we might be doing is returning to a familiar situation, but WE have changed we ARE different. We have a new consciousness and wisdom. We can bring some new energy and awareness back to an old environment. Your contribution will be different this time and you will take away different knowledge and awareness.

Another reason an individual might be going back to an old environment is to reconnect and then move on, or expand. It is a good thing to SUSPEND judging the path we are on, trust your 90%er. There could also be unfinished business in the old environment.

***

CHOICE

At that deeper inner level of you, the soul level a choice has been made to awaken and the human might not have a clue you decided that. Things will start to happen to tip the human off. To keep moving forward in this process we have to **stop blaming**, stop blaming anyone for anything we have in our life it was always our choice.

For some reason we created it and maintained it. We might not remember WHY we chose it or why we are keeping it, so we convince ourselves it is being forced on us by an outside force or entity.

Releasing BLAME is key to entering the new energy.

JUDGMENT needs to move on down the road.

Build lots of self esteem or SELF LOVE.

When you are teaching or guiding yourself or others through the awakening process remember no blame or judgment and have lots of compassion for yourself. That is what is needed to experience transformation into the New Energy and your own divinity.

There are several ways to get in touch with your divinity or soul.

I AM that I AM is good if you have that going on FOR YOU.

Communication with your inner child can be the catalyst to your soul. The soul awareness or inner child or the nurturing of a healthy mother energy is what supplies the SECURITY and SAFETY that allows the smooth transition into you trusting in your divinity, your divine self, to take that leap of faith.

TAKING FULL RESPONSIBILITY for what you have CREATED FOR YOURSELF. When you can do that the mission you picked for yourself shows up or possibly you are already doing what you came to do.

Now when the human or sometimes the soul holds back, resisting or not able to trust. Then you get a human that is aimlessly wandering around in fear and denial or else they are in pathological busyness or avoidance afraid of their enlightenment or ascension.

Now when the human says "I choose enlightenment" ascension or any of those things they have already arrived. Walking backward in time, they decide to ascend and just need to go through the steps to get there. A physics of the universe but not necessarily an understanding on the human level of awareness of all that is involved.

You are choosing how to experience your own ascension and your own reintegration with your soul. It has already happened because you decided as a creator what you wanted to do. As you walked backwards you get to decide if you want to do it easy or hard.

There is not a destiny or a predetermined path for your ascension. You aren't bound by ancestral or personal karma to ascend one way or another. The creator can choose how they want to experience their ascension.

The choice is the creators and that would be more the soul's choice than the human choice. The human choice gets to be, "Can I accept this gracefully and joyfully?" or "shall I go kicking and screaming?" Do you want to experience it abundantly? Do you want to experience it with good health? Have you been at a great feast of awareness and stolen the scraps?

Search and destroy **VS** search and harmonize.

Every time we deal with and have overcome a fear as a result of our wisdom and knowledge *we have won*. Over coming a fear is the manifestation of a **solution**. When you harmonize the other side gains new understanding. Our thoughts can change our biology.

There is NO SUCH THING AS the darkside, it is only an opposing force to keep duality balanced. The human that focuses on dark, will get dark. The more intense the focus the more powerful the dark. The same thing happens with the light. The amount of focus on light will produce that amount of powerful light.

Light is interdimensional. When light enters you it reflects many dimensions of your soul.

Light is ACTIVE, dark is **passive.**

When the light is turned on all hidden things in the dark are exposed to being seen. When you move to the light you are moving an energy framework (human consciousness). Your personal energy body is always filled with a combination of light and dark. When you add light, dark spills out. The dark part will plead, "don't leave us behind", we have been there for you lifetime after lifetime after lifetime and you embraced us then. Your dark will go into survival mode.

Your dark knows you well and will "play you".

DARK is *actually an* INTERDIMENSIONAL *layers of our DNA.*

Spiritual energetic protection is a RELIC of old energy, based in covert fear.

When you emanate your light the dark gets transmuted. As you vibrate higher light is automatically generated. So you can use your light to saturate anything that is inappropriate for you. Light is not invasive its neutralizing. Those that carry dark around by choice can no longer influence the people and things around them and create fear.

Our dreams are extremely complex and can be viewed from three different perspectives.

Biologically we are releasing our memories and rewriting them.

The brain will move things around for easier prioritizing and storing of information. While this is happening we might get a bleed through of what is going on but generally can't make much sense of it.

Psychologically your memories are prioritized **by your fears**, loves, PASSIONS and *addictions*. The brain moves things non-linear past and future are all mixed up. Things that do not go together do get put together.

SPIRITUALLY with the coming of the new energy and ascension the probabilities have greatly increased and changed. We are actually rewriting the past stored in our DNA. As we have new spiritual awareness' we can rewrite the emotions and the energies around events in our life. The mother abusing her son can be viewed as a karmic agreement.

The biological and psychological aspects are *subordinate* to your spiritual plan. Now we can interpret our dreams in a spiritual light.

Addictions and compulsive behavior are used to avoid enlightenment. In order to stop them you need to clear the fear. Relax your fears from pastlives around the danger of having spiritual information. It is safe now and will not get you killed in most countries.

Ask your soul what is needed to start the process of becoming interdimensional and vibrating higher or some call it ascension.

Do not look for a third dimensional answer. Start working on creating your own answers, look for **synchronicity** happening in your life. Your passion and a changed consciousness will move in and change your life. This will happen in stages, as each level begins you will work with it until the next stage starts. Everyone's path is somewhat different. This will be a work in progress for the rest of your life.

Creating SOMETHING from nothing is simply *changing energy*.

Use remembrance and ENHANCE it to create. Eventually that creates a *new reality within you*, taking you out of the third dimension, helping you to expand in the now moment.

God is slow and the wisdom of revelation is slow.

When we wake up at three in the morning it might be because parts and pieces of our DNA are being stripped away and reactivated. With the Harmonic Concordance of November 8 and 9, 2003, a quantum, interdimensional event signaled permission to rewrite our Akashic records and the crystalline sheath of our DNA. We were to change our vows to the vow of MASTER HOOD activate our creatorship and our divinity.

The earth is measured every twenty five years to check the humans spiritual development. 1987, was the last measurement and 2012, we are due to be measured next.

Co-creation is SPIRITUAL RESONANCE.

The secret of co-creation is in subtracting with interdimensional sight. The zero is the magic of interdimensional math which is in a base-12. Zero is the POTENTIAL of all that ever was, is or can be. Zero is variable depending upon the equation. Zero removes what is not needed and reveals the solution.

Co-creation is when you are harmonizing and amplifying and creating with another energy that has its own uniqueness. Be as unique as you wish while creating. Then be quiet and **listen** to the *song around you*. That is the musical key you are being asked to sing in. This is how a third dimensional human goes multidimensional.

The GOALS of co-creation are *peace*, **spiritual awareness**, JOY, *a long healthy life* and *sustenance*. If you think abundance is something you hoard you have not understood that it is sustenance, abundance is sustenance.

<u>ABUNDANCE</u> is sustenance. Poverty and abundance are the same thing. Abundance comes when you are alone with yourself and acknowledge your divinity. When you open up and realize that everything is complete in the moment. The moment is filled with healing, wisdom and compassion that is abundance.

***

There is no longer any prophecy around our reality we are creating our reality as we go, that is ABSOLUTELY new. There is not one entity on the other side of the veil who knows what's going to happen on this planet.

Our guides, our entourage are an infinite numbers of changeable energies that function in a goruplike fashion. The group is part of you forever. We feel the groups presence they are not numbered. They are energies not entities. The guides exist on both sides of the veil. They change when the human changes.

Duality works overtime to keep the human isolated so they can make independent choices and not be swayed by the group we belong to. All part of the earth test.

"The veil", isn't someplace, its a dynamic energy that surrounds our very consciousness and every cell of the body. It distances us from ourselves, our invisible parts.

"Lifting the veil" means turning on the light of REVELATION.

Your choice and intent to know more about what is real and what is not. With increased light comes more RESPONSIBILITY and *increased power* and **new tools** to master. Once you become accustomed to and accept this new way of thinking, you take on more of multidimensional qualities the veil has kept hidden.

You will find yourself drawn to places that alter your own perception. You are becoming a conscious creator. You are now taking responsibility for your own life. Giving your energy and responsibility away to others for YOUR LIFE is no longer appropriate. It is time to take responsibility for creating your own reality. Do not allow a leader or spouse or parent or child to create on your behalf. That time is over. You are the only one who can take responsibility for your very own perceptions and expectations.

Our expectations and perceptions create our reality as conscious creators. Anytime we are unhappy with our creation, **choose again.**

See the *possibilities* NOT the realities.

In the last fifty years the earth has tripled its population. More humans reacting to three times more humans. The governments that tried to offer the most good for the largest amount of people didn't do well. The prosperous systems are the ones that promoted self actualization and self-determination and religious freedom.

Sweeping over the planet is a consciousness of individuality.

We create our own fears so it should be easy for us to come up with a resolution for what we created.

For most this is NOT our last lifetime, this is our job, this IS what we do in the universe. We are universal professional humans. We are in love with the earth. When our life ends we just change energies and become part of another human's guide soup, part goes to the other side and part reincarnates.

THE conglomerate THAT IS YOU *is always working.*

Each of us is surrounded by our own group of ourselves. They know exactly what you have been through. They stand ready to lead you in one direction or another, if you would allow it. Recognize you have the choice to ask for their guidance if you would like it.

✳✳✳

Your STORY

The soul is an overview of all that you are, the entire system of "you", the "I AM", the higher self, the part in direct communication with God. When you can take responsibility for the illusion you created for yourself that cancels out any possibility of you being the victim. If you were the victim that was your choice. You can always choose again.

You absolutely created ALL of what you have.

It is not wise to compare yourselves to others. A rich person does not have the most, they just need less.

We CREATE our reality from our beliefs. A belief is an **electromagnetic** wave form. Our beliefs evoke our emotions which in turn drive our creations. It is not WHAT we have, it is what we THINK about what we have. When you think you do not have ENOUGH that becomes a judgment. You have created a belief of lack. When we THINK we lack we get SCARED or fearful.

If you perceive life as limiting and think there is not enough money, food or love available for all, you connect to life out of fear and **compete** for everything. If you have faith in the harmony and balance inherent in the universe you realize its not necessary to compete because there is an infinite number of things and possibilities. There is enough for all.

"Will I ever get ALL I need."

"Can I go on without it."

How about, "Everything is just perfect as it is."

Combining an emotion and belief together of lack is very powerful and draws to you experiences to prove your belief. When you believe you have lots of caring relationships and success and money. You are abundant until you sabotage it or things change.

The distance in your consciousness between lack and abundance is tiny. It is not about DOING SOMETHING. It is all about *SEEING the probabilities* of what you have currently and **not the realities**. We need to BE the abundance. The abundance of compassion and joy, fun, flow and laughter created by YOU the creator. Know you cannot make anyone love you, all you can do is *let yourself be loved.*

Stop judging someone or something as GOOD or bad. All you have created is a gift FROM you. WE are energy and consciousness expressing itself in the third dimension.

You are a sovereign god or goddess, and if lack is what you want to learn MORE about, you go for it.

Life is about loving WHO you are. Knowing you have enough to live your life with grace. Be aware of your feelings, there are no wrong beliefs or feelings. Rather than holding onto your fear of change or lack, can you move to a space of exciting expansion?

Emptiness is the First step to going within. With repeated practice you will find emptiness a comfortable serene, enlightening, and natural state of mind. Everything you need to say or do will come to you once you have emptied. Only when open and empty and listening can you receive wisdom and knowledge and learn your next move.

When you cling to an old idea, thoughts, beliefs or perceptions, you plug up your mind and stop the flow of new ideas. An empty mind attracts infinite wisdom. Throughout your day remember the nature of your mind is to be free, empty, clear and relaxed.

Silence regenerates your energy and revitalizes your whole system. With silence there is less need for approval of others and more compassion for yourself and others. Wisdom is an insight you know is right in your gut though you can't give a rational explanation.

Our challenge is to be less concerned with linear time and more concerned with staying clear and focused.

Clinging to your thoughts of pain and suffering is exactly like clinging to your thoughts of pleasure and joy. Clinging to any thought only brings more of the same. The more you attach to something, anything, the more you think it separates you from all else.

My spouse beats me, and I need to put up with it and not tell anyone because he "needs" me. How attached and isolated does that make you? I can assure you that the beatings will continue with that sort of reasoning.

The greater your attachment the more dependent you become on that attachment to define who you are. Many people have been fearful so long, their fears defines how they live and who they are. The quicker you own your fears, the sooner you can transmute them. When you do not own them you cannot change them. Shower your fears with the clear water of love and acceptance avoiding the murky water of denial. When you look within, you face your fears and move beyond them or embrace them, make friends with your fears.

Your fears have information to impart.

Kabbalists have always frowned on self-denial and self negation.

There have been times when people felt the way to truth and enlightenment was through suffering and denial. But their efforts created an attachment to self-denial they used it to define their piety. Thinking they were special separated them from others. The self righteous think themselves better because they suffer more than anyone else.

Accept what is. Start *loving your limitations.*

Knowing others is wisdom. Knowing yourself is enlightenment. Lao Tzu

As we journey the world of emotions and desire try to create peace within yourself. Accept your life as it is with joy. The option is to be not so happy because you judged and saw lack, perceived lack.

Have you noticed that for every NEGATIVE encounter you have, there is an opportunity for you to make it a positive possibility.

When we dwell on past mistakes we cling to energy that can be put to better use. Why you could be making a new mistake with that energy. Forgiveness has already occurred it is waiting for your anger and shame to subside so you can see the forgiveness. The refusal to forgive yourself or another congests the mind and constricts your energy flow.

When your energy feels depleted is it because you have used it up in clinging to your point of view and your fear of losing to the competition. Does your point of view define who and what you are? Will you be less if you allow another to do it or think it their way? When you release your attachment and return to the flow of your divinity your energy will return to you.

Can you listen without judgment?

Can you act without needing to change another.

Can you accept without analyzing, and empower without intimidation.

All the variations of experiences here are for us to become more intimate with ourselves and our life on earth. We came to experience, *not control others* and force them to "do it our way".

Even and especially children need to be on their path and not used by an angry or lonely adult.

True love is free from expectations and empty of preconceived notions.

Infinite love surrounds us at all times but at times we turn away from it.

Your sense of freedom depends on the state of emptiness that exists within you. Be liberated from your expectations for you and others, we all know what we need and want to do. Your perceptions of what is true can be very limiting to others and probably yourself too.

Though you may not complete the task you started you are not absolved from beginning it. Once you take the first step the invisible realm assist you in walking you forward. Go with a beginners mind be innocent of negative perception and emotional blockages. Again that is YOU limiting you!

During periods of confusion, remain open and calm.

In insulting another you insult yourself for it is *your own defect* that is being revealed. When you choose to stop and pick up bits and pieces thrown every which way, it is hard to maintain focus. Your decisions are right for you when they access your unique talents and serve goodness. You are responsible for seeking your own image of God; no one else's image of God will do.

As long as you cannot know what God knows, you have FREE WILL.

Once *you know what God* knows you no longer need free will.

Whatever exhausts you exhausts those around you as well.

Whatever exhausts you overworks your guides and angels. When you overwork your resources, you lose what you are trying to gain. Working in union with the universe is effortless work and joyful service. Your life DOSE have value so do not waste it any longer in the fast paced life of the third dimension of illusion.

To be free means to be free enough WITHIN YOURSELF to risk change. When you place conditions on yourself or others you are not trusting in your or their ability to know they are God and You Are God Also. This RESTRICTION causes the attachments and clinging that lead to pain and suffering. Moving from one center of being to a new one is part of growth and change. Freedom means being at peace with the fact that change is inherent in life. Freedom is a result of your inner spirit and belief system.

First we make the choice to accomplish something.

Then we go back in time to manifest it step by step.

Those that **do not make a choice** don't know where they are going and consequently *they wander aimlessly.*

✳✳✳

COMPROMISING

In duality we often compromise our energy and mind so much that the individual appears to be stubborn because they do not know which direction to go. We fragment and split ourselves when we are not true to ourselves. The time for compromise is over. Searching outside ourselves for answers is compromising. We need to be true to ourselves. In the new energy when you hold back because you are compromising, it will be exposed anyway.

Looking outside yourself for answers makes your energy drop which puts you back into old energy, duality. Some sections of humanity in the world have a consciousness of dark and shamefulness. They have created a place to dump problems and the world does not need a place to dump their problems anymore.

We each need to handle our own problems.

When you find yourself returning to an old energy situation remember you are returning to it a changed human, one with more enlightenment. You might be going in an effort to gain a consciousness and wisdom you did not have before. You might want to catch a different perspective.

You do not go back into an old energy situation to judge people and events because that will not serve you.

No more compromise about working only for the money. Now success is found by moving into your passion. Going from the human brain to the heart. Succeeding through hard work is old energy. The feeling of joy creates the connection to your 90%er and the cosmic connection. Feel the sensitivity between the two of you. In reality it is a new type of sensitivity and try not to take it personally. Take the connection objectively, rather than a personal sensitivity that way it becomes a tool for your use instead of a cross to bear.

How to make your soul proud of you, master "mastery" which is taking something that **has become negative** in your life and finding POSITIVE uses for it. That is the process called mastery.

Mastery is when you are not fearful and you are peaceful when others around are not, you do not do drama. A human's first reaction is to fight when provoked. A master's first reaction is to check herself to see if her integrity is in place. No compromising, become the master.

So you have lost a job, spouse, friends or home how do you put a positive spin on those events.

No spouse or friends enables you to get closer to yourself and go within to talk with your soul.

No job probably means you were not following you passion or soul desire, see how lucky you are to of lost that job? You were messing up and you got straightened out. How lucky are you?

No place to live opens up all sorts of options to you you wouldn't of had if you had a place of your own.

Life on earth does not have to be difficult or a struggle. That is a personal choice or you are viewing events from not the best point of view. Any time you are not happy with your choice or reality. Have the courage to choose again that is the real magic. Choose do not compromise.

As you get into the cosmic flow through your soul it connects with all things, rocks, and the animals, and all dimensions of all beings including all of the unseen world. The art of graceful acceptance is not an easy lesson. Just smile, accept and it will be very exciting.

Any energy that comes through that connection, you feel it as **passion,** you feel it as JOY. Remember that your success in the higher vibrations is directly proportional to the amount of joy and passion that you can experience on a daily basis.

Understand that you have the power to CREATE *your own reality.*

With that power comes the **responsibility** of creating FOR you FIRST, the highest reality. Take that responsibility seriously and begin creating something in your life that you are *passionate* about, that makes you happy. Something that creates *energy for you* that allows you to be of a little higher use to the universe. Creating passion around you is how you become the highest use to the universe. Things will effortlessly manifest for you.

Right or wrong are illusions that only exist in the third dimensional reality which you are now leaving. Whatever you choose is your choice and all choice is honored as is no compromise. But also understand that if you wish to step forward and you are feeling restrictions that is because you are CHOOSING to FEEL restrictions from which you can benefit. Find the "benefit" and the gift in your restriction and the restriction becomes your gift.

As in all gifts it can only be kept as it is given away.

That is when the mastery process takes place.

That is when you begin using things that have been negative energies in your life for positive purposes. That is when life gets interesting and fun. Gaia is acclimating herself to the new connection that she has to the universal energy. You are part of the earth and she is a part of you. It is a time to be led by your soul.

Assimilate the art of graceful acceptance.

We are responsible for creating a comfortable lifestyle for ourselves. Find and develop our passion even if it is only in small ways at first. We are divine humans we are already there. Claim it now!

Responsibility is the precursor to true power and humans find power scary. Those going to seers and visionaries to get answers do that because they are afraid of taking responsibility for finding the answer within. Your responsibility is first, to self. The greatest responsibility we have is our own happiness. When two people can walk side by side, not leaning on each other, but sharing their life together that is ideal. That is responsibility for your own energy. We are moving into opportunities to understand ourselves as creators.

Our first responsibility is to ourselves within our own energy field. To place yourself in a safe environment and care for your biology. We need to find joy in all we do and think. When you have taken care of yourself. Then look objectively at the other energy fields around you and rather than taking them on as your responsibility you can offer compassion and help them assimilate what they experienced. Help pick up the pieces lovingly and do not take responsibility for it.

The moment change is experienced in your life, you will see wide fluctuations in the humans reactions to it. As with Gaia there is not a gentle slow movement toward hotter or colder but wide fluctuations. As Gaia raises the water temperature the earth will vibrate at a higher rate. Even though these are very minute changes at this point, they are making big changes in the weather patterns on earth and will continue to do so. Not a gradual movement, it will swing back and forth.

Fear is only a lack of information, that is why I am sharing as much as I can.

Getting comfortable with the expansion of time and space is one of the joyful things humans get to do at this stage in their lives. Invisible realm will be there with joyous laughter to help us REMEMBER that it is a GAME we are all playing.

You might discover how your own expectations are creating your reality more than you have ever experienced before. Imagine for a moment that everything in your world exists *in many dimensions simultaneously.* Then your EXPERIENCES would be determined by which dimension YOU WERE IN and which point of perception you viewed events from.

In the unconscious world of duality choices were hidden from us. What changes and choices we did experience happened slowly and linearly. The probabilities have greatly increased and are coming much faster.

You put your keys where you always do and today you cannot find them. A few weeks later your granddaughter who is an interdimensional Crystal child says, are these what you are looking for, and holds up your keys that you have been missing. You had put them into another dimension of time and space that you are not familiar with, but your granddaughter is.

The soul at its highest level is *pure* LIGHT and ENERGY, directly connected to the pure source. You are not separate from the soul and the soul is not separate from God.

Are you one of the lucky ones waking at 3 am? Try to adjust to it as it could become the way of things. In the triad of sleep, you will generally sleep for three hours, wake for two and return to sleep for three more hours. The two hours of wakefulness can be very special because you are in an enhanced state of creation during those hours. You are in an altered dimensional state. In those two hours what you hold in your thoughts will manifest in your reality very quickly.

You do not control the thoughts entering your mind but have complete control over which thoughts you allow to stay. Keep the thoughts that add to your quality of life. Let the negative thoughts flow through they are a needed part of the human experience. Just know that negative thoughts can travel through your mind without attaching.

***

The BODY we Have

Clearing our body of stress and wounds or blocks can only be as successful as we are at keeping our life around us in the flow daily. Since manifestation is occurring more quickly now, staying joyful will help you enormously as we rediscover ourselves.

Our meridian system is a combination of energetic (auric) meridians AND the *physical pathways* of our **nervous system**. Preventative maintenance is the best way to go. Keep stress to a minimum, eat and drink pure foods, exercise and sleep regularly. If you are not doing these things it will take some work to get into new habits. The nervous system clears itself naturally when we sleep. A daily half-hour "nap habit" can create better health.

 The final chakra pair in the 8-chakra system is the third eye and soul purpose (6 & 8). Eighth chakra is your Higher Self connection, paired to your center of higher intuition. Their connection is vital to conscious ascension beyond the human form. Once the seven chakras within us are cleared, balanced and fully connected to the eighth all around us, the conscious cosmic connection is regained.

Illness symptoms can come from imbalance elsewhere in the body.

When you have an abdominal issues the throat needs clearing also. With lower back pain work on the shoulders also, as that is an example of imbalances in chakra pair 2 & 5. You can often see a thyroid cancer spread to the lower abdominal area.

Crown and Root are a chakra pair. When one falls ill, the other compensates to maintain the body's overall energetic balance. Cancer is an extreme example and easy to track. Pair 7 & I, Crown and Root, where certain cancers metastasize from brain to rectum.

The new energy enters our dominant side the hand and foot. Then the energy rises up and circles around the crown. Then descends down the non-dominant side, pushing ahead of it the old, dense energy to be released from the non-dominant hand and foot, which is the Normal Pattern.

Circling around the head acts as a circuit-breaker for the Crown to prevent blockages from lodging there. At the top of the meridian system is a circle around the head so if pressure backs up it can't go further. That is why strokes can occur in that region. After years of built-up pressure from blockages in other parts of the system. Every twinge, pain, or dysfunction in the body happens for a reason. When there is no physical evidence, the blockage is still etheric.

For example:

A pressure can form in the thigh with no discernible injury, yet knee surgery twenty years prior to that has left a meridian blockage that eventually prevents the thigh meridians from releasing downward past the knee. The thigh tissue may be sore to touch, or feel hot, yet not show any diagnosable or treatable problem and the knee is symptom-free yet it is the culprit.

The aura DOSE clear itself regularly. It has a built-in way to flushes pressure from the meridian system through our physical nervous system. All damage to the body can be released in noninvasive ways.

Fear and anger has a SPECIFIC **vibration** that dampens the IMMUNE system, interfering with proper digestion. Getting angry affects your body chemistry for SIX hours sending it plummeting.

Joy is a specific vibration that HARMONIZES the body towards its *perfect pitch*. Laughing over something for a minute boosts your body chemistry for six hours.

The physical *rewiring and clearing of the body* has had to go from the OUTSIDE *in* to prevent harm to us.

During the first, five-six years of the shift, we received NEW *spiritual guidance*.

The next five-six years, we assimilated the new spiritual concepts on the mental level.

The third, five-six years from 2000 forward we were clearing the emotional level including the heart as of 2004.

The last, five-six years of the shift our bodies are clearing on the physical level. We are feeling pressure on the lower chakras. The legs are heavy the energetic connections are not as quick or easily accessible as they used to be. The energies are causing our physical core to feel the need to release pressure. We are feeling poorly, tired, finding it hard to focus or think too long. Chronic aches and pains are flaring up. Our reality seems to be getting heavier and denser, we are clearing the patterns of illness from our *electromagnetic fields*.

The nature and flavor of orgasm has changed, and will change again in a few years when sex will change again and become deeper and more sacred than you have ever experienced. In terms of energetics an orgasm is the highest level of energy, the closest to God's that our physical body can tolerate.

Our dense etheric body is composed of the physical core surrounded by energetic layers of emotional, mental and spiritual levels.

The more we clear our density, the more we will be able to link into our heart through love, and experience sex from above the belt which is very different. Sometimes, the disparity between people's energies is enough to make them "bounce off each other" and seek different partners. If you are drawn to someone from the heart, your sexuality will flow surely and sweetly. and sex will then transport you beyond anything you currently know.

Orgasm created in the belly does add energy into the sacrum area, our energy storage spot and it does replenish your energy, maybe as high as the 3rd chakra if that is cleared enough to receive and then runs down your legs and your energy feeds the ground. You keep part of it and give part to the earth.

When all seven chakras are integrated and you are working from heart as the fulcrum that orgasm literally runs up your spine instead. Heart brings it up through the top of the head through the crown, and it comes back down, feeding your aura in a beautiful rush of energy.

OUR HIGHER SELF

The higher self functions as a big river with little streams. Each higher self manages around twelve life threads at a time. Each over soul manages a dozen higher selves at a time. The sacred mathematics of 12 x 12 = 144. A soul family is about a "gross" of souls, just like a gross of beads. When one life ends the energy is feed to another life energy, on one of the threads. No energy is ever lost or wasted!

The physical core is the smallest part of us. Our aura is "knitted" into your physical core through the energetic meridians that actually tie into your nervous system through your skin. The clearer our nervous system gets the more sensory information we receive from the higher realms.

The Veil physically connects to our body through our right brain in the eighth chakra, Soul Purpose.

The real "doing" of ascension is achieving "Oneness" within yourselves.

Now is the time to live your faith, embody and embrace the idea that there is life after life as you know it.

The planetary rise is shifting our DNA. In clearing first you release the layer of current stress from the day or the week. Beneath is the chronic layer, where your old whiplash may rise up all those old familiar aches and pains. Beneath that layer is the genetic, pastlife level, which clears the DNA of pastlife traumas, faulty belief systems, and inherited illness patterns. Our body is using about *25% of your physical energy just to shift itself.*

It is time to take responsibility for changing what you can in your own life. So many people suffer from sleep deprivation, and don't realize it. Many people suffer from dehydration which can lead to migraine headaches, and they don't even realize their body needs water.

The second big barrier to healing is old, faulty belief systems. Biology follows our beliefs. Your total being vibrates at the level of your thoughts and feelings about everything. Unconditional Love is the highest level of energetic emotion you can feel. Fear in all its faces comprises the lower half of the vibratory emotional scale. Love heals and energizes, keeping the body young.

Take responsibility for where you are, gather as much information as you can about your symptoms, and then search for the medical and holistic tools you are comfortable with.

Make PEACE with your **limitations**, find joy in each little moment, no matter what your situation is. It is a question of mind over matter find peace of mind and nothing else matters.

Find THE GIFT in all that happens to you and you change your reality instantly.

When you reach your journey's end and have not been joyous throughout the goal itself the PRICE WAS TOO HIGH to be fulfilling.

***

Evil is what damages love in the self or others.

Fighting evil means there is an evil energy you must eradicate.

FIGHTING evil IS the energy you focus on so it must be in your aura.

When you resist evil, it will eventually win your full attention and affect your life temporarily. Evil is temporary, light will flood in and heal you.

A belief is a thought you think repeatedly.

Energy follows thought.

The truth is simple and clear.

Everything is god, humanity is experiencing different levels of remembering the truth at this time. The clearer the memory of self the more light you hold the more light your aura holds.

God is creation and her creations are growing and expanding. Once set into motion that life keeps growing and evolving. God is ALWAYS creating as an expression of love.

May you live in unity peace and joy and NO you do not lose your individual divine personality including your individuality, your passion, excitement, growth and adventure.

People who prefer the finer things in life prefer people.

We are **one mind** with *many thinkers*.

SIGNS OF STARTING THE ASCENSION PROCESS MOVING INTO THE NEW ENERGY.

Some part of you has said "bring it on" usually not a part talking to the human.

I.   **Crying** and crying and crying for no present time reason. Tears are good they release old energy and stuck energy. Your DNA is being updated and that causes **aches and pains** in the body more intensely felt in the neck, shoulder and back.

2.   A deep **inner sadness** for no present time reason. Your current and past lifetimes are coming to the surface of your awareness to be listened to, blessed and released. Its hard to say good bye.

3.   As we move from letting the brain dictate our behavior to our heart we start **losing things**: jobs, spouses, houses, family, friends, things like that. We are in transition and getting in touch with our heart our feelings.

4.   **Sleep patterns** change and change again. You might awaken around 3 AM ish because of work going on within you when you can't go back to sleep get up and do something. Dreams of war, being chased or of

monster are energies of the past that are coming to be blessed and released.

5. Frequently our body has a hard time keeping up with all the changes. **We forget** what we are saying and doing as we move from being brain centered to heart centered. We drop and misplace things a lot. This is not a time for multitasking do only ONE thing at a time. Spending more time in nature will help ground you and calm you so you can get to know the new you.

6. Talking to yourself or your 90%er increases. You may feel alone and removed from others because you are. You are walking the lonely path of spiritual awakening and filling your immediate space with your own divinity. You made the final choice to do this and now you are walking backwards through it or time. It is a series of choices or sequences that build one upon the other.

7. No desire to do anything so don't. You are in the void or holding your soul's hand. You might feel suicidal because you have completed your karmic cycles. You are ready to begin a new lifetime while still in this physical body.

8. In and around all of this you will have periods of cleaning and straightening the space around you. Getting rid of many things you do not use and have hung onto that no longer serve your changed self.

✻✻✻

1987—2012

   During the first five-six years of the shift, we received **NEW** *spiritual guidance.*

The next five-six years we ASSIMILATED the new spiritual concepts on the mental level.

The third five-six years, 2000 forward we were clearing the emotional level including the heart as of 2004.

The last five-six years of the shift our bodies are *clearing on the physical level.* We are feeling pressure on the lower chakras. The *legs are heavy* and the energetic connections are not as quick or easily accessible as they used to be. The energies are causing our physical core to feel the need to release pressure. We are feeling poorly, tired, finding it hard to focus or think too long. Chronic aches and pains are flaring up. Our reality seems to be getting heavier and denser, we are clearing the patterns of illness from your *electromagnetic fields.*

The nature and flavor of orgasm has changed, and will change again in a few years when sex will change again and become deeper and more sacred than you have ever experienced. In terms of energetics an orgasm is the highest level of energy the closest to God's that our physical body can tolerate.

Our dense etheric body is composed of the physical core surrounded by energetic layers of emotional, mental and spiritual levels.

***

OLD ENERGY WAYS

Old energy needs *two opposing forces* to create new energy. It is confusing and challenging to maintain balance in the middle of these two opposing poles of energy.

In **duality** we are exposed to deceit, self deception, corruption, greed, and decadence. Duality, opposition was encoded in our DNA. We setup this vibrational FRICTION on purpose to increase our wisdom and understanding. Generally speaking we made the ratio of energy in duality 1/3 to 2/3.

New awareness happens VERY slowly.

The same amount of energy kept being recycled. Law of Conservation of Energy is it can neither be created nor destroyed. Energy can only be converted from one form into another. Third dimensional **time and space are linear**.

The biblical era is ending.

A large number of birds and some animals will be leaving as their time of service with us is over, they want to go home.

The illusion of duality and FEELING OF separation also presented a close small picture of reality.

Carbon based body that cycles rapidly.

Energy is linear, if you do A and B you always get C no matter what the bias is on the experimenter is.

The old pattern was, create anything you needed through THOUGHT and **very hard work**.

Our creating became a battle of outsmarting and outwitting the competition. You told yourself to *stuff your fears*, be **strong and positive**. DENY anything that might get in your way. Instructors set down rules and conditions as defined in lesson plans. Have tests on what was learned. Imagination has been ignore and considered a weakness.

Miracles are drama.

Passion was based on duality and very limited. The imagination realm can be uncomfortable—they let ANYONE in.

Business felt the *end justified the means* to increase profits. The energy goes in only one direction, right to the bottom line. Each worker had an hourly wage tied to them. She is a nine dollar an hour, pink collar person. The equation too frequently is WIN—LOOSE

Owners chose the bottom line as their priority NOT the work force. Jobs are boring and limiting, workers were not honored.

In old energy things went on rather **slowly** and outcomes were *easily anticipated.*

We split ourselves up into ACCEPTABLE and **unacceptable** parts. WE expanded the brains job description too large for it to handle.

Invisible realm cared for and watched over us.

In the spiritual area the invisible realm taught about the many worlds the soul may enter and how to travel in the soul body.

Visualization is old energy and from the brain NOT very creative.

Our future had been created by us living in our thoughts of what tomorrow would bring and that was appropriate.

✳✳✳

SOME THINGS WE CAN KNOW ABOUT NEW ENERGY

New energy comes into the individual ALTERING the **body and mind**.

It is good to allow the new energy to move through our entire body NOT JUST THE MIND. The changes are rapid as is your awareness'. Instead of turning to the Bible people will go inside themselves for answers, JUST AS JESUS DID. We are inside of God a oneness.

New energy is INCORRUPTIBLE.

New energy is the new quantum interdimensional physics. It is expansional and there is an infinite supply of energy available to us.

There is "no time", only NOW interdimensional time. Compassion and the giving and receiving of unconditional love is a state of timeless serenity. The new template is that everything is perfect as it is and there is no effort or struggle needed any longer.

There is enough **abundance and compassion** available for *everyone*.

We are slowly evolving into a silicon body because it is more flexible and lighter. Our carbon based bodies get threaded with silicon which acts more like the new energy. This process starts when you are in the void and your awareness is increasing.

New energy is nonlinear and when you lack understanding of the way it operates it appears chaotic because it takes into consideration your wishes, BUT cannot be controlled or force or contained. It is expansive and moves in and out of the many dimensions. Up to a point you can literally plot new energy and chart it mathematically .

Our DNA loops are all being reattached and will begin working together again as they have before. As they do that it will help us to heal all of our past scars and wounds within our body and auric field, physically and emotionally when we are living in the divine NOW moment.

Though the creator feels fear and self doubt we understand those emotions are real and present and we own them. These energies do not need to be considered **negative** they can work with you and for your creations.

Instructors of spiritual understanding need to know it can be done.

IMAGINATION is the intelligence of the new energy. Imagination is used to create with. The imagination realm is a higher vibration and safer because only those with compassion and love can "hang" there.

Passion is expansive and open to many new realms. **Passion is LOVE EXPRESSED.** Passion is fuel and is expansive and moving in all directions open to many new realms.

New energy goes in MULTIPLE *directions* which is beyond our current consciousness.

The new energy business to succeed has to have *consciousness and creative thought working hand in hand*. The money shows up as a result of your creativity, compassion and honoring of all those involved. The new energy business will be physical, spiritual, compassionate and creative *all at the same time*. WIN -WIN -WIN—WIN—WIN

Consciousness needs to be alive along with a creative pool of energy expressing itself in many directions. Spiritual consciousness is moving into business and all the people involved.

Create from the heart.

Things are going on so rapidly and in so many different directions we MUST meld all our rejected aspects into **one**. Allow NEW energy to entire all areas of the body and embrace all PARTS of you that you have rejected.

Invisible realm needs us to be sure to share with them all we learn and feel as they are learning after we do for the first time. We are putting it together for them and need to check frequently that they know what we are doing. We need to keep our entourage informed about what we are doing and changes that happen.

The divine humans stay where they are and **expand** out to any person or place they might want to interact with. Instructors of spiritual understanding need to know it can be done.

In oneness there are no opposing forces.

Our creative powers and abilities in the new energy are expansive and almost unlimited. Our opposing DNA loops will be melded and working together again as our 90% and 10% start to combine.

FUTURE REALITY is an **assimilation** of awareness from **ALL** the **HUMANS** and their vibrational frequencies.

***

BOOKS BY BONNIE BAUMGARTNER

website **mysticknowing.com**

1. <u>Healing Self-Defeating, "Nutty" Behavior</u>
So you or someone you know is a lunatic. Everyone has bad moments but some people have bad lives.

2. <u>It's All about Loving Yourself</u>
What you might not know about the illusion we are living in.

3. <u>Love or Trauma: and Heal Multidimensionally</u>
Many abused children grow up not knowing if they have been subjected to or are delivering abuse or love.

4. <u>Joyfully Being a 10%er</u>
More commonly known as the human

5. <u>Keep It Simple</u> Mystic Knowing
We are divine beings in human suits with rather limited awareness of our spiritual connections.

6. <u>E_x p a N D i n g</u>
Into Other Dimensions the Ascension Process.

7. <u>DIMENSION SURFING</u>
1,2,3,4, and ALL THE REST of the dimensions at once.

Made in the USA